D0401495

She was trapped with no hope of escaping!

Selina gazed at Luke in consternation. The weight of her dilemma overwhelmed her.

Should she go with him—a stranger determined to reach some secret destination, who might implicate her in serious trouble before he finally discarded her? Or should she return to her unwelcome suitor—waiting to force his attentions on her, who would penalize her mercilessly for the trouble and publicity she had caused?

"Which is it to be, Selina?" Luke asked softly, his clear gray eyes holding hers. Slowly she felt the tension ebbing, and it was as if he had put a protective wall around her.

Her voice barely audible, she answered, "I'll go with you...."

Other titles by
ROSE ELVER
IN HARLEQUIN ROMANCES

1949 — SHINING WANDERER
2054 — FIRE MOUNTAIN

Other titles by
ROSE ELVER
IN HARLEQUIN PRESENTS

245 —GOLDEN APPLES

Many of these titles are available at your local bookseller
or through the Harlequin Reader Service.

For a free catalogue listing all available Harlequin Romances,
send your name and address to:

HARLEQUIN READER SERVICE,
M.P.O. Box 707, Niagara Falls, N.Y. 14302
Canadian address: Stratford, Ontario, Canada N5A 6W2

or use coupon at back of book.

Tiger Sky

by

ROSE ELVER

Harlequin Books

TORONTO • LONDON • NEW YORK • AMSTERDAM
SYDNEY • HAMBURG • PARIS

Original hardcover edition published in 1978
by Mills & Boon Limited

ISBN 0-373-02244-1

Harlequin edition published March 1979

Copyright © 1978 by Rose Elver.
Philippine copyright 1979. Australian copyright 1979.
All rights reserved. Except for use in any review, the reproduction of utilization
of this work in whole or in part in any form by any electronic, mechanical or
other means, now known or hereafter invented, including xerography,
photocopying and recording, or in any information storage or retrieval system,
is forbidden without the permission of the publisher. All the characters in this
book have no existence outside the imagination of the author and have no
relation whatsoever to anyone bearing the same name or names. They are not
even distantly inspired by any individual known or unknown to the author, and
all the incidents are pure invention.

The Harlequin trademark, consisting of the word HARLEQUIN and the
portrayal of a Harlequin, is registered in the United States Patent Office
and the Canada Trade Marks Office.

Printed in Canada

CHAPTER ONE

SELINA ROXLEY recovered consciousness slowly. She felt hot ... so hot ... and there was a dull, bruised ache all over her body ....

She groaned as she became aware of the sun beating down on her like a powerful white light burning red through her closed eyelids and scorching the skin of her face. Her right arm was flung out to one side and she could feel stubby new turf beneath her fingers, but her left arm appeared to be wedged awkwardly under her. Moving in slow motion, she raised her free arm to shield her eyes, and lifted her heavy eyelids.

She was in a small clearing surrounded by a sea of waving elephant grass; lying partially on her back with the lower part of her body twisted over from the waist down, as if she had stumbled and collapsed clumsily and made a futile attempt to get up before losing consciousness. Beyond the thick, towering grasses mountain peaks hung on the horizon, a jagged, purplish mirage against the hazy sky. A drifting speck overhead lowered into the circling wing-span of a vulture or a marauding kite hawk leading her eye to the dense tree-tops of the jungle in the distance.

Selina closed her eyes and groaned again. The weight of her arm on her forehead was painful; she shifted it slightly and found the touchy spot— lumpy, tender, probably a bruise. Where was she?

And how long had she been lying like this? she wondered dazedly, making an effort to remember what had been happening and why she was here at all.

It was some minutes before it began to come back to her, long minutes while she was overcome by nausea, and sweat beaded her lips and ran down under her arms, and the buzzing of flies merged with the buzz in her head.

She was in the Corbett nature reserve in the Himalayan foothills: somewhere in hundreds of square miles of forest and scrub jungle. She had despaired of escaping from the clutches of her stepmother, Delia, and the repulsive, frighteningly persistent attentions of the man Delia was quite determined she should marry. But she seemed to have succeeded, because she was entirely alone.

So much was clear—the rest surfaced slowly from her fuddled memory.

It had been Henry Spencer's idea that they should spend the chilly, blustery months of English spring weather abroad; he, she, and his sister Delia, petite and soignée and ceaselessly watchful, to keep an eye on her. He had offered a Mediterranean cruise, then a cruise on a yacht in the warm Caribbean, but in spite of Delia's nagging and threats, Selina had flatly refused. Undaunted, his large black, curiously expressionless eyes fixed on her with hypnotic insistence, Henry had then suggested a trip to India, to one of the national game parks, and Selina had rather foolishly given in. Delia, with a swift, knowing smile at him, had been satisfied.

As the preparations went ahead Selina had had her doubts, but she was weary of resisting the two of them and it promised to be a distraction, a respite.

She had seen films of African safari parks and had visualised the travelling, the wildlife, the evenings sitting around a camp fire while a weatherbeaten game warden recounted amusing or exciting stories of his experiences. India would offer the same sort of vast, open-air environment, but with a different, unfamiliar landscape. She wondered how Delia would stand up to the lack of amenities and shrugged the thought aside. She, Selina, would revel in it. And she would be free, not cooped up with Henry and Delia most of the time as she would have been on a yacht. As she always was even in her own home.

It began well, but hadn't worked out that way. Henry had hired a limousine to be at their disposal on arrival in Delhi, and for a couple of days Selina had been lulled off her guard in the pleasures of sightseeing around that historic city with its intriguing mixture of Western modernity and the smells, sounds and vigorous bazaar-bustle of the East.

They had cruised along the spacious thoroughfares of New Delhi, seen the President's palace and gardens, the grandiose public buildings and sweeping circular colonnades of the central legislature. They had visited the Lal Keela, an ancient fortress with massive red walls and ornamental marble pavilions in one of which had once stood the legendary jewelled Peacock Throne of the Moghal emperors. They had explored the exotic little shops in the street market called Chandni Chauk, then driven south to gaze up at the seven-hundred-year-old Kutb Minar, a remarkable free-standing tower of red sandstone and marble soaring into the sky.

Selina was enthralled by it all, old and new, and noting that her usually haughty withdrawn manner

had changed to sparkling enthusiasm, Henry had
eyed her with silent satisfaction. Later that evening,
as they had dined in their expensive hotel, he had
promised a special trip to Agra, on their return
from the nature reserve, to see the matchless beauty
of the domes and minarets of the Taj Mahal.

The following morning they had set out to drive
across the northern plains towards the Himalayas,
the three of them in the limousine followed by a
jeep hauling a trailer to transport the Indian servants and the quantities of food and baggage Henry
had considered necessary to make their holiday in
the nature reserve 'reasonably civilised', as he had
put it ... which, as far as Selina was concerned,
seemed to defeat the whole purpose of a jungle
safari.

However, she had had no serious qualms as the
miles swept by, being too absorbed in glimpses of
the harsh simplicity of Indian village life, the convoys of lumbering bullock-carts, the smell of dust
and the bleached glare from a cloudless sky on the
browns, greens, ochre and saffron yellow of a time-
less limitless land. They had crossed the rippling
grey expanse of the river Ganges, then on to the
teeming industrial town of Moradabad from where
they had branched off on the route to Ramnagar.

As they entered the nature reserve along one of
the lesser, fair-weather roads, civilisation melted
away in shadowy sal forests, heavy jungle thickets
and stretches of tall, elephant grass, and by the time
they had arrived at a rest-house, some thirty miles
from Ramnagar, the sense of isolation had been
complete. Henry had booked the place exclusively.

Selina shut her eyes tight and pressed her knuckles

to her trembling mouth. What a fool she had been! Too late she had realised that this rest-house was the end of the line for her. She had been duped; she was a prisoner again, as Henry and Delia had intended. Cut off from all contacts now.

Apart from a singularly unsuccessful early-morning jaunt perched up on the back of a tame elephant, to try and see some wildlife, there had been no suggestion of camping or trekking or visiting another jungle rest-house in the reserve. Delia had explained, in a die-away voice as she lay back in a cane chair and fanned herself languidly, that she really didn't feel at all well; and when Selina had icily suggested that they should return to England, the woman had reminded her in a sharp voice of the money she and Henry had already spent on her. And that the least Selina could do was to co-operate by going on short expeditions with him and keeping him happy.

But Selina had no intention of going alone with Henry, whose black basilisk eyes and clammy touch made her flesh creep; and he had no intention of allowing her to go exploring on her own either. She was not even allowed beyond the compound because of the possible danger from a wandering tiger or wild elephants and for three days she had fretted at the inaction, tired of trying to elude Henry and humiliated by the thought of having been trapped so easily, her mind busy with various hare-brained ideas for escaping the merciless pressures he and Delia were putting on her.

Then what seemed to be a more practical notion occurred to her. There had been a railhead at Ramnagar, where they came into the reserve, and if she

could somehow purloin the jeep and get away on
the Ramnagar road it would not be long before
she could board a train, find her way to Delhi and
fly home. Henry had obviously instructed the Indian
servants to keep an eye on her and the cars in the
daytime, and her only hope was to bribe one of
them lavishly to help her at night.

It had been easier than she expected; the rustle
of ten-rupee notes from her store of currency and
travellers' cheques had persuaded one of the servants to push the jeep silently down the track from
the rest-house in the small hours of the morning;
then she had thrown a few clothes and essentials,
her money and passport into a light case and crept
out into the eerie dawn to find the jeep.

There was no alternative but to trust the servant,
and he had been there, waiting by the jeep. He had
pointed out in broken English and with many
gestures the direction of the motor road, pocketed
the money she had promised him and vanished in
the shadows. She had sighed with relief at finding
the ignition key in place, switched on and shot off
along jungle track at breakneck speed, tense with
fright and a feeling of desperation.

Small wonder that it had ended disastrously in
an accident, Selina acknowledged wryly to herself as
she released her left arm and flexed her fingers
tentatively. So much tension and uncertainty, and
fear of the deep, brooding jungle shrouded in half-
light. It had been an unnerving experience, foot
down hard on the accelerator as she raced against
time and against the panic that gripped her whenever she heard the cry of some prowling creature
disturbed by the noise of the jeep.

She could remember emerging from the track, swinging on to the road and careering along with reckless abandon. Every now and then she had cast a glance over her shoulder expecting to see Henry's car burning up her trail. As the luminous dawn-light spread, she could remember thinking that there should only be a few more miles to go to make sure of her freedom, and yet being vaguely disturbed by the fact that the rough road seemed to be climbing slightly instead of levelling down.

And then, in a couple of crazy seconds, it had happened ... a careless glance back just as a herd of spotted deer broke from cover almost under the front wheels of the jeep. She had swerved and braked, and felt the jolting impact against her head. She had spent some time slumped over the wheel, her mind a blank until it was filled with the urgency to get out of the vehicle and hide ... somewhere ... anywhere....

Clutching her reeling head and dragging her feet, she had pushed and stumbled her way through thickets and banks of thick elephant grass until she found herself staggering around a small clearing of burnt-out stubble. The urgency drained out of her, the effort had been too much; there was a dull pain in her knees as she fell on them and pitched forward.

And now ... Selina moaned and wiped the sweat from her upper lip with a shaky hand ... she was stranded, and in pain, and only God and the hot sun overhead knew exactly where she was! Moving warily, testing her muscles, she was relieved to discover that her body and limbs appeared to be functioning normally. Except for a splitting headache, some bruises and red-raw scratches, she was capable of getting back to the road—if she could find the way. But driving on, going to Delhi, was beyond hope.

If she could get as far as the jeep and wait they would come and pick her up before long. Henry would have set off after her as soon as her disappearance became known when a servant took in her *chota hazri*, the 'little breakfast' of tea and toast served early in the morning. Yes, Henry would be there, fixing her with his unblinking, reptilian eyes, telling her how foolish and headstrong she was in a soft, cultured voice which always chilled her with its menacing insincerity; and Delia would probably be there too, bottling up her stinging accusations and reproaches until they had returned to the confines of the rest-house.

Selina covered her eyes again and swallowed convulsively, her mouth dry at the thought of facing them and brazening it out. After this abortive escapade the pressure would probably become intolerable, making it impossible to keep up a front of cool, haughty resistance. They would remove her passport and money. And there would be more brutal reprisals in store for trying to thwart their plans for her.

Well, it was all up with her now ... or was it? The sun was so high!

Selina lifted her arm, squinting against the sun to look at the watch on her wrist. It was unbroken and the hands showed that it was close on noon. Eight hours! Eight hours since she had escaped from the rest-house, and at least five hours since they would have found her missing. Another hour or two to come upon the abandoned jeep and search around for her. . . .

Surely they should have located her by now? She could hardly have strayed *that* far from the road, not in the dazed state she was in. Why hadn't they caught up with her yet?

Puzzled, she creased her brow, and winced at the bruise, but a faint renewal of optimism stirred the dreadful lethargy weighing her down. Perhaps there was still a chance of freedom if she made it back to the jeep. And provided that the little runabout wasn't damaged, and she had enough strength left to handle it for a few miles . . . a few more miles. . . .

Selina made an attempt to sit up and failed, shutting her teeth tight on the nausea and disappointment. Why hadn't they come to fetch her? she thought querulously. The way she was feeling even Henry would be better than this utter helplessness. What would she do if nobody came? It would get worse as the hours passed, and after dark —what would she do then? There were roaming animals—she had forgotten about the animals— and hook-tailed scorpions, and worst of all snakes, deadly snakes. They were all around her now. She was sure of it. She could sense it and was terrified.

She went rigid in every muscle and her stomach contracted. She could hear the breeze hissing in the grass—was it the breeze? She must think, *think*, how to get out of this mess. If only her mind was clearer and she had some cold water to slake her thirst and bathe her throbbing head.

The rustle of the grass was getting louder, but it was almost drowned by the drumming of her heart. She was in such a state of panic by this time that when she felt a hot breath on her ear and something like a soft wet nose against her face she flung out her arm and screamed. There was a yelp as her hand struck a hairy body and she screamed hysterically again and again. Then the barking started, and the din of screaming and barking almost split her head open.

'*Patch!*' roared a voice. A resonant, masculine voice—and gloriously human! The sudden release from fright was so great that Selina choked and then fainted.

When she came to, she could hear a murmur of talk. Water was trickling on to her dry lips and she put out her tongue to draw it into her parched mouth. There was also a blessedly cool damp compress over her forehead and eyes. Raising her hand, she moved the pad and found herself looking into a rugged, sunburnt face with strongly contrasting golden brows and sun-streaked hair, and eyes of a pale, hard flint-grey, very deep set, which looked back at her as if he could see right into her brain.

'How do you feel, Miss Roxley?' the stranger asked.

'How do you think?' she retorted, petulant because her head was aching. 'What kept you?' She had to steady her lips, her whole body was trembling with reaction. 'Did—did Henry send you to look for me?'

His brows quirked up. He glanced across her and she saw a handsome, middle-aged Indian in an immaculate drill safari jacket, kneeling on the other side of her. And beyond him a black and white mongrel squatting forlornly on its haunches, one ear pricked, the other flopped forward, regarding her with liquid brown eyes. The man turned to her.

'Who the hell is Henry? Was he with you in the jeep?'

'Of course not.' She took a deep quivering breath. 'No—no, I thought you were a game warden or something. I thought he—he might have hired you to look for me.'

'Nope.' That grey-eyed gaze was watching the fleeting expressions on her face. 'I'm Luke van Meer and this is my friend—er—Narayan.'

The hesitation was noticeable, and she said suspiciously: 'Then how do you know my name?'

'We were driving west up the track when we spotted your wrecked jeep. Your case was still in it, and your passport in the handbag. It took a few minutes for Patch—the dog—to sniff you out.'

'Oh-h-h ...!' She shut her eyes again on a deep sigh.

He said: 'That's enough talking for the moment, you must have taken a pretty nasty crack on the head. We're going to try and get you back to the road where I have a first-aid kit.' He began to run his hands over her arms and legs and body, and in any other circumstances she would have struggled and pushed him off, furiously indignant, but she suffered it in silence because his touch was completely impersonal.

'Are you a doctor?' she mumbled, flapping away an insistant fly.

'Of a sort,' he sat back on his heels. 'You don't seem to have broken anything, so I'm going to give you a fireman's lift. Okay?'

She nodded weakly, content for the present to leave things to the two men. Later ... later she

would have to think for herself and decide what to
do.

With Narayan's help Luke van Meer got her into
a sitting position and then up and over his shoulder,
and she was surprised how gently both of them were
handling her, but when they set off through the
elephant grass and the scrub jungle she moaned with
pain from her hanging head and Narayan came
round to place a hand against it to keep her steady.

They passed the jeep, tilted at an angle with the
front bumper buried in the dry, crumbling earth
of one of the large anthills near the road, then on
towards a small car, its roof rack so laden with
bedding-rolls and other gear that it looked like a
ludicrous dung-beetle. They laid her down gently
on a grassy verge, and while Narayan fetched an old
cardigan out of the car and folded it to put under
her head, Luke van Meer rigged up some sheeting
between the car and an adjacent bush to give her
shade. Then he got a first-aid box out of the crowded
boot and started cleaning up her scratches and
bruises.

Selina's black cotton cord jeans had been badly
ripped when she had scrambled her way frantically
through thorny scrub, and she had to press her lips
together to stop herself crying out at the sting of the
surgical spirits Luke van Meer was using on her
delicate white, lacerated skin. When he had covered
the cuts on her arms and legs with adhesive dressings he gave her an anti-tetanus shot.

She was grateful, but still fretful. 'Do you always
carry a portable surgery around with you?' she
asked sourly as he dabbed the spot with spirits. She

was not wholly convinced yet that Henry hadn't
sent him.

His mouth quirked humorously. 'Just a Boy Scout
at heart. Be Prepared, that's me.' He tidied her
jeans and red checked shirt. 'We always carry one or
two essentials, and a few extras needed around here
—drugs for malaria and dysentery, anti-venom for
snakebite, things like that.'

He began tending the bump on her forehead,
just above her eyebrow, and although she winced
she was impressed by the quick competence of his
big square hands. Selina looked up and met his eyes
as he applied a dressing, securing it in position by
winding a bandage round her thick, silky mass of
chestnut hair. She must have been mistaken about
that flint-hard acuteness in his eyes. His gaze was a
bland, smoky grey with a suspicion of amusement.
What was there to laugh about, for heaven's sake!
she thought crossly, shutting her long curling lashes
against him.

'I hate to have to tell you this, Miss Roxley,' the
amusement was in his voice too now, 'but I think
you're going to have a juicy shiner.'

Her lids flew open. 'You m-mean a black eye?'

'That's what I mean.' He put things away and
closed the first-aid box. 'What's—er—whatsisname,
Henry, going to say about all this?'

'You *are* from Henry!' she accused him wildly.

'Relax, will you?' he ordered, his light tone hard-
ening suddenly. 'I told you—no! But I guess he'll
have to know what happened soon.'

'Not if I can help it!' she responded so fiercely
that his eloquent brows shot up.

'You can't hide those bruises. Well, we'll talk

about it reasonably when your headache's better and
your temper has improved.'

She turned her head away, tears pricking her eyes.
This whole day had turned into an almighty dis-
aster. He had rescued her, done so much for her
already. She said stiffly: 'I'm sorry, I didn't mean to
sound churlish, but you don't understand. . . .'

'Who understands women?' He had reverted to
mild amusement. 'Okay, I'm sorry too. Here now,
let's prop you up a bit.'

The arm around her shoulders was firm and
reassuring, lifting her. Narayan was standing beside
them holding an enamel mug. While Luke van
Meer had been patching her up the tall, silent
Indian had got a Primus stove going and boiled
a tin kettle and made some tea. Luke van Meer
gave her a couple of analgesic tablets and she took
the mug, murmuring thanks, and gulped them
down. The strong tea had no milk but was liberally
sweetened and tasted like nectar. Selina had had no
food since the previous night and became aware of
gnawing hunger but hadn't the courage to ask if
they had anything to eat. She wondered where the
men had come from and where they were going.

Narayan gave her another mug of tea and as she
swallowed it thirstily he said: 'You look better,
Miss Roxley. It is fortunate that this mishap occurred fairly early in the year. In another few weeks
you would have been quite dehydrated lying out
here in the hot sun. Heat stroke, you know.'

'Yes,' she owned miserably, thanking him for the
tea in a small voice.

The two men left her to rest for a while and drank
their own mugs of tea as they examined the jeep for

damage. Selina heard snuffling and found the mongrel inching along the ground towards her on his
belly. He pawed at her tentatively and she looked at
the melancholy brown eyes and ran a finger over
his foxy muzzle, whispering: 'All right, you found
me, so you're forgiven for frightening the life out
of me, but how am I going to get out of this fix?'
At which he whimpered in reply and she felt like
having a good weep. Her rescuers were conferring
quietly, too far away to be overheard. Discussing the
jeep ... discussing her ... she drifted into an exhausted doze.

When she awoke her head was still sore but she
felt much more able to cope. To her surprise she
saw that her companions had the jeep back on the
road. It looked undamaged!—that was encouraging.
She lay watching the two of them as they stood together talking. A strangely ill-assorted pair. Luke
van Meer was a big, rangy individual with blunt,
bronzed features and untidy hair; very casual, even
slovenly, in the way he wore his loose-fitting drill
slacks and a sweat-marked bush shirt. Not a bit like
the tall, impeccable figure and aquiline brown face
of his Indian friend.

Selina's mind was now clear enough to start con-
triving a new plan for herself. The jeep seemed to
be serviceable. Those two Good Samaritans had
done all they could for her in the circumstances,
and as Henry hadn't employed them she could tell
them she was going on to Ramnagar and ask for
some food and directions to help her on her way. It
was only mid-afternoon, she could do it easily. She
was relaxed and optimistic, floating on a cloud of

airy confidence; a prisoner reprieved at the last
moment!

She sat up warily—a little stiff and tender but
not too bad, she thought—and called: 'Mr van
Meer!' Both men looked her way. 'May I have my
bag and a little water to freshen up?'

Luke van Meer lifted her case from the jeep and
strolled towards her smiling lazily. 'When a woman
starts thinking about her appearance it has to be a
good sign!' Putting down the case, he went to his
car and fetched a water bottle, then walked round
the back of the nearest bush, beat about for a
moment and came back. 'Safe enough for privacy
there,' he said.

Selina found her handbag tucked inside her case,
and also took out a small towel. Luke helped her to
her feet and she retreated out of sight and managed
fairly well, although she felt a bit faint and had to
drink some of the water. Her reflection in the mirror of her compact showed a white, drawn face with
bluish streaks already appearing around the edge
of one of her large, long-lashed violet eyes and
her bandaged head added to her woeful appearance.
She covered the bruises with foundation and
powder, touched up her pallid cheeks with blusher
and put on some lipstick.

Her hands were still very shaky, and the prospect
of setting out on her own in the jeep once more
brought weak tears to her eyes, but she blinked
them away and returned to the men, determined
to see it through somehow. To her chagrin, her
knees were wobbly and she had to flop down again,
making a pretence of stowing her towel and bag
in the case. Luke van Meer's critical appraisal

added to her misgivings, but she took a deep breath and said loftily: 'I do hope the jeep's all right. I'd like to get to Ramnagar by this evening.'

'Would you indeed!' was the satirical comment. 'Is that why you were going the other way?'

'*Going the other w-way?*' she jerked her head back in consternation and felt a stab of pain. 'Oh-h ... no-o-o!'

'Oh, yes. By the tyre marks and position of the jeep you were headed for the hills, Miss Roxley.'

'I couldn't have been!' she wailed.

But she could; and she knew it. It had been dark and she had been terrified, and she could have turned off on to the wrong track. That would explain why Henry and his minions hadn't caught up with her in all these hours! They must have been searching the Ramnagar road, assuming she had taken the main route out of the reserve—as she had had every intention of doing.

They would probably still be there, making enquiries, hunting around for their quarry as they would hunt for an escaped animal. Henry would probably have a check made all the way to Delhi, and the chances of her getting through now were non-existent.

The last, fragile vestige of renewed hope died. Selina buried her head in her hands.

'Oh, God!' she whispered. 'What am I going to do now?'

CHAPTER TWO

Luke van Meer stood with his thumbs hooked in his belt watching Selina's dispirited figure crouching at his feet, noting her delicate, ringless fingers and the lustrous tawny glints in her dishevelled hair above and below the bandage around her drooping head. For a moment his eyes were narrow and thoughtful, then he glanced at Narayan's impassive face and shrugged and said testily:

'Pull yourself together, Miss Roxley. We're not likely to leave you here in the middle of nowhere to fend for yourself.'

His barely concealed impatience stiffened her shoulders as nothing else could have done. Her head came up with the haughty tilt she always used on Henry, and her round, thickly lashed violet eyes surveyed Luke with a cool, supercilious stare, full of bravado.

'You and Mr Narayan have been marvellous and I'm grateful, but I'm sure you would like to be on your way again. Please forgive me if I've delayed you, but don't let me keep you any longer.' She brushed off a fly nonchalantly. 'I still have the jeep and I'll work something out.'

'Don't talk rubbish,' was the forthright response. 'That clout on the head must have been worse than we reckoned if you imagine you can get by on your own. Were you running away to this man Henry in Ramnagar, or were you deserting him after a row?'

He saw the sudden compression of her lips and added tersely: 'Either way it was a damn silly stunt for you to go haring around in a jeep without any protection or sense of direction.'

There was a short, fraught silence until Selina found her voice, saying haughtily: 'If you've quite finished, Mr van Meer, please go.'

'You can't dismiss us like a couple of servants, Miss Roxley.'

'Oh-h, heavens!' she cried distractedly. 'You know I didn't mean it that way. Once you've gone perhaps I can begin to think more clearly.'

Luke van Meer went down on his heels beside her. 'Look, it's my guess you've run out on Henry from a rest-house in the reserve, am I right?' His tone was brisk but more persuasive now. 'Whatever the reason, it would be wiser to go back. Tell us which one and we'll see you get there safely.'

She couldn't let them take her back into the trap, not now that she was feeling battered and confused and weak for lack of food. To be confronted by Henry and Delia together, without the strength to withstand their onslaughts, was past bearing. In a way, she thought hysterically, she would rather die.

'I don't remember,' she improvised, touching her head.

He heaved an exasperated sigh. 'Come on, Miss Roxley. Narayan and I have a good way to go before making camp, and we haven't the time to tote you round a hundred and twenty-five square miles finding the right place.'

'I'm not going to any of the rest-houses. The only thing I want is to get out of the reserve somehow, get to Delhi and fly home to England.'

The Indian interposed quietly: 'Alas, we cannot spare the time to escort you to Ramnagar, nor can you travel alone in this condition. Besides, your family or friends will be extremely worried about your safety, is it not so?'

'Oh, yes, they'll be worried all right,' her voice broke on a bitter little laugh, 'my ... my so-called friends! But not for the reasons you're thinking.' She was frightened and swallowed hard. 'Safety! In many ways I'd be safer out here alone....'

Luke stood up and said abruptly: 'What was the trouble?'

'The trouble was that I was gullible enough to allow them to bring me to this isolated nature reserve in the first place,' she said bitterly.

'That figures,' he drawled with a sardonic edge as he took in her rather tattered slender elegance, the delicacy of her manicured hands, the almost classical beauty of her face which anxiety, bruises and bandages couldn't disguise. 'You're hardly the type for roughing it.'

'I'm tougher than I look.' The blusher stood out in contrast on her cheeks as her colour receded. She clenched her fists. 'I've—I've had to be.'

'What does that mean?' Luke's brows came down in a harsh line when she averted her head. 'You said you'd be safer out here. Are you alone in the rest-house with this man Henry? Has he been pestering you?'

'No, I've not been alone with him,' she admitted, but her voice shook with repugnance. 'Delia's there.'

'Who is she?'

'My father's—wife.'

'Your stepmother? Why isn't your father there too?'

'Because he died last summer—and she's no kind of mother to me, nor ever will be!' she informed him emphatically.

There was an interminable pause, then Luke said sceptically: 'Are you saying that this man has been molesting you, and your stepmother does nothing to prevent it?'

'Must we go on with this inquisition! I'm not saying any more—except that I'm not going back to them.' She closed her eyes and breathed in a spent voice: 'You're like everyone else I've ever tried to talk to....'

'Try me with the truth.'

Selina raised her head and for a long moment Luke's gaze held hers with such hard grey cynicism that resentment surged through her veins in a hot tide and broke through her frail defences.

'You can take that sneering look off your face, I know what you're thinking! I'm a spoilt brat—I'm bored—I can't stand the rough life! I've had a fight with my boy-friend and I'm creating as much trouble as I can for everybody concerned!' Her face was scarlet with anger, making the skin of her cheekbones taut, dry and painful with the beginnings of sunburn. 'You want the truth?' she flung at him shrilly, 'I'm scared.' A hammer was pounding inside her head and her voice dwindled. *'I'm scared!'*

The Indian looked shocked and looked away. Luke turned on his heel, took Narayan by the arm, and the two of them retreated along the road to the jeep leaving Selina sitting on the ground with her hand over her eyes, struggling to regain her composure without bursting into tears.

She had not cried since that day her father had died and she was not giving way to it now although the accumulation of months of strain was there, behind her eyes, ready to flood out. There was something crawling on her other hand and she jerked nervously to flick the ant away. As if sensing her distress, the dog nuzzled close to her. She stared down at him, concentrating on the irregular white patches on his back as she fought down the tightness in her throat. Men were all the same, she thought bitterly—here was a mongrel, a skinny pi-dog with more instinct for genuine fear and unhappiness than all of them put together.

It took her some time to rally, slowly accepting the fact that she would have to give in to Luke van Meer sooner or later. She sat stroking the dog for another minute before turning bleakly to call out to Luke and tell him she had resigned herself to going back. He was still talking to Narayan, out of earshot. The Indian glanced her way, then said something to Luke, who nodded and came striding towards her.

Selina straightened up and began to scramble awkwardly to her feet, but Luke caught her shoulders and lowered her gently into a sitting position again, going down on his heels to be on a level with her.

Before he could speak she shrugged his hands aside and said wearily: 'I don't think I can take any more, Mr van Meer. You win. I had no right to impose on strangers, and if I've seemed rude and unreasonable——'

'No, Miss Roxley, you've won this bout.'

'—it's because I was feeling so shaken up I couldn't think straight.' Her head came up slowly, her eyes widening into a large, round bewildered stare. '*What* did you say?'

'If the situation, whatever it may be, has forced you to such drastic lengths, we'll have to do something about it. I'm sorry I put you through the hoop rather harshly just now, but we had to make sure there was more to this than a giddy little adventure that went wrong.'

She searched his face apprehensively, scarcely daring to believe what he was saying until his steady gaze and serious expression convinced her. She had to shut her eyes as the sudden feeling of release made her head swim, slacking her tensed muscles until she swayed back and would have collapsed if he hadn't put a hand behind her neck and gently propelled her head forward between her knees.

When the faintness passed she lifted herself, unconsciously pressing against him, whispering: 'Thank you.' This time he cupped her head, tilting it up and putting a small silver hip-flask to her tremulous mouth. She took a mouthful of neat cognac, choked on it and sat coughing while he rubbed her back vigorously, a contrite grin softening the lines in his lean cheeks.

'Another sip?' he offered when she recovered her breath.

'No! ... no, thanks. I'm so empty I won't be able to hold it.' She pressed a hand to her midriff as the scorching warmth spread through her.

'When did you last eat?' he enquired in a brusque tone.

'Last night ... dinner, of sorts. I didn't feel much like it, I was too worked up about the chances of getting clear. And this morning I sneaked out before dawn, and I couldn't think of anything except whether the *kansama* wanted the money enough to risk moving the jeep down the track for me so that I could start the engine without giving myself away.'

'You were bribing one of the servants to assist you, Miss Roxley?' said Narayan. How long he had been standing quietly near them Selina had no idea, but he seemed very concerned and she nodded:

'I had to. Henry was paying them to see that I stayed in the compound and it was the only way. But he gave me the wrong directions, or I was too jittery to take it all in ... I don't remember.'

'We'd better not delay any longer,' Luke clicked down the top of the flask decisively.

Selina looked from his face to the Indian's and back. 'What ... what are you going to do?'

'Get you out of harm's way for a start. I take it your obnoxious swain, Henry, is beating the bushes for you all the way to Ramnagar and beyond, but he'll have the search widened when he draws a blank, so the sooner we get moving the better. Narayan and I can't afford much more delay either.'

Feeling guilty, she said: 'I didn't mean to hold you up for such a long time. But I'm glad it was you who found me ... I mean, I could have been completely lost, or it might have been someone else less ...' she stumbled for a word, 'less scrupulous.'

'How do you know we're not unscrupulous?' was the bland comment.

'I don't,' she snapped with a return of spirit. 'I'll

have to take it on trust, won't I? I have to trust somebody.'

'The gullible Miss Roxley, on your own admission.'

She glanced uneasily at him and saw the twitch of humour on his mouth which belied his tone. Still light-headed with relief, she said with pert condescension: 'You're all I've got, and a jolly sight better than being lost in this—jungly place. I shall make use of you for as long as I can.'

'Brandy talking!' he observed dryly, but there was a glint in the grey eyes. 'Come on, this is no time for backchat.'

He rose to his feet in one agile movement surprising for such a big man, and before Selina knew what was happening had swept her up into his arms. Narayan moved ahead, a slight smile on his lips as he opened the passenger door of the car so that Luke could deposit her on the front seat. As the door closed on her Selina fetched a deep sigh, still incredulous about the sudden turn of events. It was warm and stuffy inside the small car and she laid her head back, eyes half closed.

Luke van Meer was right, she thought, trying to rouse her faculties. She was very foolhardy to trust herself to a couple of complete strangers. They had spent a long time talking it over—talking *something* over. They could be abducting her for all she knew, planning to get money out of Henry for her safe return. They had come to her rescue, but she had no idea who they were, what they were doing, where they were going. She ought to have asked ... questions ... pertinent questions before....

It hardly seemed to matter. Was it 'better the

devil you know'—back to Henry and Delia? Or the
devil she didn't know—yet? For some unfathomable
reason she felt secure inside this stuffy little car and
her choice was not really in doubt. Luke van Meer
had decided and Selina was content for the moment
to leave it to him.

He eased his hefty frame into the confined space
behind the wheel and tossed the sheeting, and the
cardigan which had been used to support her head,
on to the back seat. As he moved round to put the
key in the ignition his shoulder and arm was like
a bulwark against hers.

She sat up. 'What about the jeep?'

He thrust his head out of the window, looking
back. 'Narayan will handle it.'

'My case. . . .'

His big shoulders turned and his mobile brows
shot up, and at the mockingly aggrieved expression
on his face she laughed, a thin quavering laugh but
the first for many months. 'Sorry I spoke!' she murmured, and found herself smiling into the glinting
grey amusement of his eyes.

The jeep rolled slowly past them, Narayan at the
wheel, her case on the seat beside him and the
mongrel sitting sentinel behind. The Indian lifted
a hand in a vague salute and accelerated away at a
good speed, disappearing in a billow of dust.

'We'll give it a minute to settle.' Luke fished
around among the maps and papers under the dashboard and took out a tin of glucose tablets, saying:
'Dissolve a few of those in your mouth, it'll stave off
the hunger and keep you going until we set up
camp.'

'When will that be?'

'In a couple of hours.' He switched on and the car edged forward, bouncing off the verge into a well-worn track. Selina felt a little shiver of expectancy, a mixture of hope and uncertainty and anticipation, as the speedometer flickered upwards, and the wilderness began to sweep past in a blur of greens and golds with here and there a brilliant splash of colour from a mass of scrub jungle or a distant tree.

They were silent in a strangely companionable fashion for some miles while she let the glucose tablets melt in her mouth and her muscles and nerves unwound in a way she would not have thought possible a day, a week, a month ago. Her mind had begun to ramble pleasantly, speculating on what the man beside her did for a living, and whether he was on holiday or duty of some kind, when he said: 'How did the accident happen?'

'M-m-m ...?' It brought her back to the realities of the situation, but she could be objective about it now. 'I was driving like a maniac because I was frightened. I kept glancing over my shoulder to see if Henry was following me and a herd of—deer, I think, leapt across in front of me. All I remember is a sort of reddish brown, and dancing spots, and I wrenched the wheel over and landed in the anthill, I suppose. I don't think I bumped them, injured any of them—at least I hope not.'

'I shouldn't think so. Narayan and I didn't stumble across any gory victims when we were searching for you.'

'It's all very well for you to mock ... but the sun was just coming up and the light was peculiar, and I couldn't *bear* to kill anything!'

'Well, you didn't and there's no call for agonies

of remorse. I would guess that they were *chital*, quite common in the reserve. Beautiful little creatures, dappled with white spots in lines along their flanks and a black line from the nape of the neck to the end of the tail. The herds are usually feeding for three or four hours after sunrise, so they must have been on the move when you came streaking along and flushed them out.' The wheel slid through his big, competent hands as the track curved round a heavy clump of bushes. 'What possessed you to wander so far?'

Her shoulders lifted helplessly. 'Shock, perhaps. A panicky feeling that I had to hide myself—get away from the jeep, from Henry, from everything. I had a sledgehammer beating on my forehead and I must have been a bit demented. When I think what might have happened if you and Narayan hadn't. . . .'

'Okay, forget it,' he said firmly, and Selina lapsed into silence again, shifting down into a more comfortable position in her seat.

She mused idly that he was much younger than Henry . . . about thirty? Her gaze moved to the steering wheel, to his capable, square-tipped fingers. She pondered on the fact that his nails were remarkably clean and well kept considering the rest of his slovenly appearance. On his forearms and wrists the hairs were abundant yet so fine that it looked as if his darkly tanned skin was flecked with gold. She had an irrational desire to run a finger over the bare arm nearest to her; an idiotic notion, soon quelled.

She swallowed a tiny yawn and wondered what time it was. Luke was wearing a heavy digital watch, an expensive one too, by the look of it, another item out of keeping with his shabbiness. Her own wrist watch had stopped. Her eyelids had begun to droop. He was an odd type ... Luke van Meer ... with an odd sort of name ... it sounded Dutch, but his English was impeccable except for a faint trace of an accent at times ... North American, not Dutch....

When Luke threw another glance at her, Selina was asleep.

Barking and the harsh sound of crows prodded Selina back into awareness and on opening her drowsy eyes she beheld a flock of these feathered scavengers, with grey caps and sleek black wings, strutting around inquisitively a short distance away. Patch was chasing the crows off in short bursts of noisy energy to which they responded with raucous indignation before returning within a few seconds to torment him.

Smiling at the pi-dog's futile efforts, Selina tried to have a lazy stretch, but winced at the movement and then lay quiescent for a moment or two watching other birds wheeling overhead against a saffron sky as they came home to roost. The air was heavy but fairly cool now. A breeze ruffled through the leaves of a grove of shisham trees. She could hear the distant lap and ripple of water and smell the tang of wood smoke.

Presently she tested the unfamiliar surface beneath her and discovered that she was resting on a low camp-cot. She hoisted herself up on her elbows. The car and the jeep were parked on one side at the foot of a rock cliff, while on the other was an orderly camp of two small tents and other gear. There was a fire crackling hospitably inside a circle of small boulders over which lay a rough gridiron with a cleaned and gutted fish on it, and nearby stood the Primus ready for the kettle.

Beyond the neat camp site the ground sloped down between bushes and rocks to a river bed of darkening water, It was all just as she had imagined and hoped it might be when she had agreed to the holiday, thought Selina, not quite sure if she was awake or dreaming. Then certainty returned as the tall, dark figure of Narayan appeared, walking back from the riverside carrying water bottles and the kettle.

He came towards the camp-cot and the crows took off, flapping and cawing, into the tree-tops. 'Ah, Miss Roxley, I see you are with us again,' he said with a quiet smile. 'Sleep is the best thing for regaining your strength.'

'I must have been completely out for the count!' She laughed a little ruefully. 'I don't remember a thing about all this.'

'Yes, you were deeply asleep and relaxed when we arrived here.' He set down the water bottles, lighted the Primus and put the kettle on it. 'You did not even stir when Luke carried you out of the car and laid you on the cot. It has been good for you, I think. Are you hungry?'

'I feel a lot better for it, and—yes, I'm starving! Have you just caught that fish?'

'Not I!' he gave her a humorous look. 'Mr van Meer is a dedicated fisherman, Miss Roxley, which is a boon to us both. He caught that *mahseer*, a splendid specimen, in a rock pool a short way along the river. Fish seem to beg to be taken on his line.'

'They wouldn't dare refuse him!'

'True,' he returned on the same light note. 'Luke can be very obdurate when his mind is set upon something.'

'Have you known him long?' she ventured casually.

'Oh, yes, a few years now.'

'He seems to know about animals.' A thought occurred to her which would explain their presence in the reserve. 'Is he—is he a naturalist?'

'A knowledgeable amateur.' He busied himself with the camp equipment and was not, apparently, inclined to elaborate.

Although Selina was disappointed she hadn't the nerve to persist with the kind of personal questions that would tell her more about the pair of them. It was hardly important, she assured herself a little crossly, she wouldn't be travelling with them long enough to make any difference. Yet she would have liked to hear a bit about Luke's background—and Narayan's too, of course, she tacked on hastily. Both her benefactors.

Swinging her legs over the side of the cot, she sat looking wryly down at her torn, dishevelled garments and grubby hands. She was tattered and sweaty and could do with a thorough clean up and change of clothes, and there were other pressing, more intimate necessities about which she was too shy to approach Narayan. He was the soul of courtesy and would help her all he could, but she already felt, quite irrationally, that she was on much closer terms with Luke. Like a—a brother, she thought, justifying the sudden need for his large, decisive presence to tell her what to do. Extraordinary, when she hadn't even known of his existence a few hours ago.

Where on earth had he got to? she wondered impatiently; and at that moment he came up the slope from the river wearing only an abbreviated, damp-looking pair of khaki shorts, a towel slung round his neck, his fair hair darkened with wetness, and his bare arms and legs still glinting with drops of water. Watching him walk towards her, she was struck by the difference in the shambling figure he presented in ill-fitting clothes and the disciplined tension of torso, arms and muscular thighs that she could see now, and became aware of a strange feeling in the pit of her stomach.

He stood in front of the camp-cot. Selina tilted her head back to stare up into his clear grey eyes. It seemed an age before she became self-conscious of her own appearance, swallowing a constriction in her throat, dragging her eyes away from his concentrated gaze.

'I'm sorry I wasn't awake to help with the chores.' It was the first thing that came into her head. Then hurriedly: 'Can I bathe too?'

'No. You look a good deal better for sleeping, but under the warpaint on your face you're washed out. I guess you've been a bit concussed, so take it easy for tonight.'

His tone was enough to shake off the disturbed sensation in which she had been caught a few seconds ago. 'I must have a proper wash,' she protested haughtily, 'and change, and there are other things....'

'Sure. There's a snug little corner which should do fine for the *memsahib*'s toilette. If the *memsahib* will graciously allow me a moment.'

She flushed scarlet at the ironic servility, and at the ghost of a smile on Narayan's lips as he bent to poke up the fire. How could she have thought that she had some special claim on Luke van Meer's consideration? Hateful, sarcastic man! She said: 'Whatever you think best,' in a glacial voice, and was far from mollified when he laughed a deep resonant laugh and said: 'Good girl.'

Luke extracted a clean but crumpled shirt from one of the kit-bags, shrugged his shoulders into it and buckled a pair of Indian *chuppli* sandals on his big feet. He produced a tin bowl and mug and picking up the hot kettle, ordered her to 'Stay put' as he carried them away behind a tumble of rocks. Narayan deposited her case on the camp-cot. She thanked him, avoiding his eyes as she selected another pair of jeans and a loose shortie kaftan of vivid cotton print she had bought in Delhi, and by the time she had sorted out a fresh bra and briefs, her wash-bag and towel, Luke had returned.

To Selina's annoyance she had to accept the support of Luke's arm to the secluded hollow among the rocks he had found for her. 'Shout if you need any help or see anything moving, I'll be waiting on the other side of that big boulder.' He took her chin and forced her round to meet his eyes. 'And no sneaking down to the river.' His mouth twitched with amusement at her cool air of disdain. 'There's a python down there large enough to crack your tender bones and squeeze the life out of you.'

Her eyes widened, she shuddered and pulled away from him. Turning her back, she arranged her garments on a rock, and when she looked again he had gone. The bowl was already filled, the kettle handy to replenish it, and if Luke had invented that python it was not worth the risk of trying to find out now! She stripped and made the best use of the 'snug little corner', revelling in the balm of the cool evening air on her skin. In spite of her experiences with Henry it never entered her head that Luke would invade her privacy. Much as she might resent being the butt of his sardonic amusement she felt completely safe in the hands of this stranger out of nowhere. It made no sense, but she didn't question it.

Towelling herself quickly, Selina put on her clean clothes with a sigh of satisfaction, deciding not to bother with make-up. 'Luke?' she called, unaware that she had dropped the formality of Mr van Meer. 'I'd like to wash out my clothes.' He reappeared with surprising alacrity.

'Here, let me get that bandage off your head.' She stood perfectly still as he unwound the bandage, inspected the bruise and tossed the bandage aside. 'The dressing will be enough. Sit up on that ledge and do your hair while I tend to these.'

She sat on the rock and there seemed nothing incongruous in soothing the tangles out of her mass of silky chestnut hair with a brush as she listened to him laundering her discarded personal garments at the waterside. When he came back he spread them on the rocks, saying: 'They'll be dry by morning. You look like a mermaid perched up there.' He stooped and fitted her expensive leather, hand-made brogues on her slender bare feet, lifted her down and, gathering everything together, took her back to the camp.

Bemused and strangely content, Selina shared the camp fire with the two men, with the pi-dog squatting expectantly beside her. She ate fish and a small juicy orange, and drank tea with crude sugar called *gûr*, and enjoyed it all with a hungry relish the most perfect French cuisine could not have aroused. The fire crackled and sparked, throwing a ring of wavering light into the purple shadows of a dream-like, self-contained world enclosed in rocky vegetation, full of the night sounds and dank smells of the jungle yet curiously peaceful. The men held a desultory conversation which told her nothing about their plans, and it wasn't until she had taken her Paludrine anti-malaria pill and sat back, while Narayan chewed *paan* made of betel leaf and areca nut and Luke lit a cigarette, that she asked reluctantly:

'What shall I do tomorrow about—about getting to Delhi, I mean?'

The tip of Luke's cigarette glowed. He blew a wraith of smoke. 'We're not far from a place called Kaladhungi where Narayan knows some reliable people who will take you by road to Haldwani and by rail to Bareilly where you can catch a train to Delhi. You have your passport, return flight-ticket and enough money to see you through.'

'How do you know that?' she demanded suspiciously, and saw the ironic smile as he said:

'I've been through your wallet, Miss Roxley, remember?'

'Oh ... yes.' A peculiar coldness ran over her skin.

'Don't worry. We'll arrange everything,' Narayan added kindly.

She was appalled to find that she didn't want it

arranged; she wanted to ask where they were going, *and ask to go with them.* It was only this false sense of security Luke had engendered, she thought, pushing it to the back of her mind as she mumbled: 'Thank you.'

Later they lighted hurricane lanterns and made up the camp-cot in one of the tents for Selina. As she crept under mosquito netting Luke said: 'Whatever happens, don't put your bare feet on the ground because of snakes and other crawlers, and always shake out your shoes before you get into them.' He held the net away, the light from the lantern etching the blunt outline of his bronzed features. He ran a light finger around her bruised eye which sent a pleasurable little shiver through her and he straightened immediately and tucked the netting round her.

'You're quite safe with us, Selina,' his eyes were clear and direct, 'do you understand me?' She nodded mutely and he said: 'Have a good night's rest, you're going to need it for your round-about journey home.'

He let the tent flap drop behind him and she lay for a long time hearing the murmur of voices beyond the banked camp fire. Then she was strangely lulled by night sounds: a rustling in the jungle, the whirr of crickets and zing of mosquitoes, frogs croaking in hidden marshes, the lonely, repetitious call of a night bird. And profound human silence.

She must have slept heavily for a while, for when a sudden wailing cry and distant chorus of yapping startled her awake she saw that the tent flap was open again, a sickle moon hung against the starry sky and Luke van Meer was lying by the fire nearby.

'Luke!' she called tremulously.

He moved slightly. 'It's only a jackal, Selina. Go to sleep.'

He was there, and she was safe. Safer than she had been in her own home or anywhere else. Safe with him.

But tomorrow ... tomorrow she would be frighteningly alone again.

CHAPTER THREE

SELINA arched her back and snuggled under the blanket, keeping her eyes shut until the unfamiliar clamour of monkeys and jungle birds and all too familiar but far distant crowing of a cock penetrated her senses. She could smell canvas around her. She blinked and opened her eyes to the dim, opalescent light of sunrise filtering into the tent.

Recollection came tumbling back with depressing clarity ... today's the day—I must get up—I must get ready to leave.

She sat up on the camp-cot, then heard the low-pitched hum of a battery shaver outside the tent flap and decided to wait until whichever of the two men it was had moved away. The sound ceased and after a few minutes she pushed the mosquito netting aside, gingerly shook out her shoes before putting them on, and ventured out of the tent.

It was a crystal morning. Dew glittered on cob-webs and the pink buds of a patch of saf-flower, and hung on the thorns and star-white blossoms of the tangle of plum bushes. The first rays of the sun struck across the grey rock cliff, shining on the lovely green of new leaves on the shisham trees and turning the motes of dust over the camp into shimmering trails. It all looked different to her eyes now; the jungle was beautiful, no longer mysterious and intimidating. She took a deep breath. She had no right to feel depressed on a morning like this. She

was going home. She was *free*! She would make sure
that Henry and Delia would never trace her again.

The fire was alight already and an old enamel
coffee pot stood on the gridiron with a faint breath
of fragrant steam trickling from the spout, but there
was no sign of Luke or Narayan. Patch sprang down
from the back of the jeep and gambolled towards
Selina, stretching against his forepaws with a wide
yawn and wagging his ring of a tail hopefully.

'All right,' she said softly to him, 'come with me
if you want,' and collecting her wash-bag and towel
wandered over to her secluded corner among the
rocks. Her clothes were dry. She folded them; they
were so torn that she would probably have to throw
them away. As for washing, there was no bowl or
water now. It was daylight and she could use the
river. Well, why not? She skirted the rocks and
went down to the sandbank with the dog snuffling
and frisking beside her.

The river ran in a sheltered jungle valley. It was
fairly shallow, flowing like smooth grey silk where
she stood, but she could hear the rush of toppling
water and glancing upstream saw that it narrowed
into miniature cascades swirling over boulders.
Then she caught sight of Narayan further up the
bank, wearing only a spotless white loincloth, carrying out some kind of cleansing ritual of his own
religion. Hastily averting her eyes, she moved away
downstream and around the rocky outcrop to another sandy bank screened by bushes beside a deep
pool.

It seemed private enough here, and the sun-
dimpled ripples were very inviting. She would strip
and swim in the cold invigorating water. She was

putting her clothing in a safe place when Patch
began to bristle and growl and retreat, and the next
moment a flat, snake-like head appeared on the
surface of the pool.

Immobilised with fright, Selina watched the head
turn, saw the protruding eyes and the long, thick,
sinuous outline undulating beneath the surface.
The python—oh, God!—why hadn't she taken
Luke seriously? Her breath was suspended. She
wanted to run, but her feet seemed glued to the
ground. Suddenly she screamed 'Luke!' wrapped her
arms around her bare breasts in terror and shut her
eyes tight.

She heard an answering shout which sent the
birds flapping and calling from the trees in alarm,
then scuffing footfalls behind the rocks. The bushes
shook and there was a loud splash of a stone in the
pool.

'Okay, okay.' Hands descended on her bowed
shoulders, pulling her shuddering form against him.
'What the devil are you doing here?'

'I was g-going to t-take a s-swim.' Her teeth chat-
tered with fright in a highly charged silence during
which the python submerged.

Luke's grip tightened momentarily, biting into
her thin naked shoulder bones. An exclamation exploded from his lips as he released her abruptly,
picked up some clothes and threw them at her. 'For
God's sake cover yourself up,' he snapped.

The hot colour swept over Selina's face. She
grabbed her jeans and wriggled into them, thrust
her head into the shortie kaftan. 'All I wanted was
to bathe and get ready,' she asserted in a shaken
voice muffled by the folds of the kaftan. She jerked

it down round her neck and over her midriff.
'Narayan was far away the other side, you weren't
around, the coast was clear. How was I to know that
—that *thing* would be in the pool!'

'You won't be told, will you! I warned you about
it yesterday.'

'So I knew there was a python around,' she retorted, trying to save face with angry bravado, 'but
I didn't expect to see it in the water!'

'The more fool you. Pythons swim, you irrespon-
sible little dummy!' He gathered up the rest of her
gear. 'It's gone now, into those rocks and trees on
the other bank. Come on,' he said roughly, 'I'll
find you a place out of harm's way.'

Seething inside at his caustic severity, Selina followed him meekly upstream. She was deeply morti-
fied at having had to be rescued again—and being
so nakedly vulnerable. Everything had looked so
beautiful, so peaceful, she hadn't stopped to think.
He wouldn't understand that she had been preoccupied with storing up a precious memory of this
little sub-montane valley where she had felt carefree
and confident for a few brief hours. The python had
jolted her back to the wry knowledge that confidence
was something you had before you knew better. All
she seemed to get out of life was unnerving experiences.

Luke took her up to the spot where Narayan had
been and put her things on a flat boulder. 'Will a
tin of baked beans do you for breakfast?'

'Yes, thank you.' She added stiffly: 'And thank
you for coming in time. I'm an ignorant nuisance,
but I won't trouble you much longer now.'

She thought he said: 'Don't be too sure,' and was

about to demand what he meant when Narayan came running up the bank towards them, hastily buttoning his safari jacket and wanting to know what had happened. Luke began explaining and the moment was lost. Luke told her offhandedly that he would change the dressings on her cuts after she had washed and the two men returned to the camp leaving her to get on with it.

As she slipped off the kaftan again and knelt under a spurt of foaming white water she saw that Patch had stayed with her and drew a vague sort of comfort from the fact that the little mongrel seemed to have a predilection for her company. Still feeling shaken, her face puffy, her skin sore, she splashed and shivered under the jet from the rock. She sat back on her heels with her heart in her mouth as a slight movement across the rapids caught her eye, then let out her breath in a prolonged sigh as she saw what looked like a family of otters paddling upstream.

This had been enough to distract her mind for a few minutes, but while she scrubbed her teeth she returned to Luke's cryptic,' 'Don't be too sure.' Could he—she cupped her hand under the jet and rinsed her mouth—could he have meant that he had decided to accompany her? Even for a small part of her journey—perhaps as far as the railway station he had mentioned? Or was he merely implying in his nasty derisive way that she would probably get into more scrapes of one kind or another before he and Narayan were finally rid of her?

Energetically she towelled herself dry and as her skin began to glow she felt a bit more cheerful. She bent and peered into the pi-dog's soulful brown eyes and confided foolishly: 'He was pretty mad, so he might have been having a dig at me, but it's possible he'll come with me, isn't it?' She tickled Patch's flop ear and giggled shakily when he squatted and curled round to scratch the spot violently with his hind paw. 'I'll miss you, you disreputable hound!' she said, and began to dress, blinking at tears from a sudden pang of heartache which caught her unawares.

The hope that she would be able to rely on Luke's guidance and protection for a while longer had been overtaken by the dispirited thought that it could only be for a very short time. They would have to go their separate ways soon. Parting was inevitable. For heaven's sake, she told herself fiercely, be realistic and face up to this! The fact that she owed her life to Luke van Meer didn't tie her to him. He was bossy enough to take charge, but only for as long as it suited him, and his corrosive rudeness was very wounding. Yet the idea of parting dismayed her, and although she tried to convince herself that it was fear of having to cope on her own, she knew it was more than that. She would probably never see or hear from him again.

So what? She combed her damp hair severely back, slipped on her shoes again, debated putting on some make-up and shrugged it aside. It scarcely mattered what she looked like. The main thing was to find out what Luke and Narayan proposed to do next—and go along with it.

Moving down the river bank, Selina approached the camp as resolutely as she could because Luke might still be in a nasty mood. He had his back to her, standing beside the fire where the coffee pot and another pan were simmering, while Narayan seemed to be packing a unit with knobs and dials into some plastic sheeting. Wondering what the technical-looking equipment was for, she also noticed that the tents had been struck, and the small car was already loaded with gear; signs of imminent departure which made her stomach contract. She took a faltering step and stopped dead at the sound of Luke's harsh, disparaging voice which sent a shiver through her.

'I don't think she has the stamina for it. She'll get ill or do some other damn fool thing and injure herself, and we can't risk any lengthy hold-ups if Bala Sen's itinerary of their movements is correct.'

'Luke, there is no alternative.' The Indian's tone was quieter but quite clear. 'Too many explanations would be needed now if we took her to Kaladhungi. They have well-organised ways of passing information to protect their routes, and one word of our involvement could jeopardise months of work.' He tightened the rope and stood up. 'Which risk is the greater, my friend?'

As she stood frozen, with her limbs beginning to tremble, Selina heard Luke swear graphically. 'If I had foreseen the complications I would have dumped her back at any rest-house! Whatever else he is, her libidinous boy-friend is thorough—a trouble-maker with money to throw around, so we can't buy him off or put him out of the way.'

'I agree.' Narayan rubbed the back of his hand along his jaw, considering for a moment or two. 'There is no time for making new plans, we must contrive as best we can. We can hire a hill-tat or a mule for her to ride where possible, and later, when the search eases off, we can send her down to Rani-khet with my most trustworthy man. Govind Singh would be. . . .'

Selina crept behind some bushes, her fingers pressed over her lips, obeying a blind instinct to hide as she listened to their incomprehensible discussion. Patch, who had been snuffling along the bank investigating a scent trail, skidded up to her and she crouched and put a gentle hand round his muzzle and clutched his collar. The pi-dog rolled his eyes towards her and sat down as if he sensed the need to be quiet.

She had missed some words but caught most of Luke's reply.

'. . . a real hassle. You can bet your bottom dollar Spencer won't let the matter rest at that. The news media will have a field day with her disappearance, and if reports get back that a woman answering her description has been seen with us they'll be on to it like hawks and blow the gaff.'

'That depends on *who* is with us, Luke,' the Indian suggested with subtle emphasis. 'The lady accompanying us is your young wife, no?' He paused. 'A few changes in her appearance would suffice, other clothes, short hair. Lying so long in the sun yesterday has burnt her pale skin and it will soon darken in the open air. Europeans often bring their wives trekking in the hills. But I ask you, would you expect a woman to be taken along to a rendez-vous such as ours? Most unlikely!' He added reflectively: 'To have a woman with us may serve to strengthen our cover, Luke.'

'The wise and wily East!' Luke gave a short laugh. 'Maybe it would work at that.' There was a

silence and Selina strained her ears. 'Okay,' Luke
conceded laconically. 'I guess it's the least of all the
risks.'

'Will the girl co-operate, do you think?'

'Leave her to me. I was the one who decided to
fetch her along with us yesterday and I'll take the
responsibility.'

Narayan asked: 'How much can we tell her?'

'As much as concerns her for now. Afterwards
we'll see how things pan out.' Luke had moved and
his voice was ominously impatient. 'She's taking a
hell of a time. I ought to go and see what's going
on.'

Selina shrank back feeling bewildered and
slightly sick. She understood that something had
mysteriously occurred to change their plans overnight. She understood that they meant to keep her
. . . but for how long? . . . under what sort of duress?
Why were they so anxious no one should find out
who they were and what they were up to?

Last night she would have jumped at the chance
of being allowed to travel with them; less than ten
minutes ago she would have been relieved and excited if Luke had offered to look after her for as
long as possible. Now their obscure, clandestine
intentions alarmed her. Snatches of their conversation scurried through her brain. How did Luke
know Henry's surname (she couldn't recall mention-
ing it) or the steps Henry was taking to track her
down? What did Luke mean by not being able to
'put him out of the way'? Kill him? . . .oh, God!
. . . not that, it was unthinkable. Her head began
throbbing. What was this secret rendezvous they
were headed for, for which they had decided to

drag her along disguised as Luke's wife to cover their real purpose. And how real would the demands of being Luke's 'wife' turn out to be?

'Selena!'—Luke's full-throated roar was enough to make the crows flap and the monkeys in the trees start gibbering.

She almost leapt out of her skin, releasing Patch who immediately barked and danced around her, giving her position away. There was no point in hiding, no use attempting to make a run for it. She straightened up, swaying a little with shock, and walked round the bushes into view, judging that it would be more prudent to rejoin the two men and pretend that she had heard nothing. Who could tell what they might do if they suspected? It would be easy enough to put *her* out of the way, and no one the wiser.

'About time!' Luke strode towards her. He extended a hand to take her arm. She flinched away involuntarily and his hand dropped to his side as he scrutinised her face through narrowed eyes.

'What's the matter now?'

'N-nothing,' she denied loftily. 'I hope I haven't kept you waiting.'

'So it's Miss Roxley with airs and graces again, is it!' he said with that infuriating glint of amusement. 'Still sore at me for bawling you out over the python?'

'No, of course not. It's just that I ... that I ....' She clasped her fingers tightly together to steady herself and saw his expression change to one of concern. Bogus concern, she thought desperately; calculated to disarm her. 'Well, seeing the python did upset me, I suppose.'

'More than somewhat, by the look of you. You're as sickly as curdled milk under your blotchy sunburn.'

There it was again, gratuitous rudeness! She bit her lip and averted her head to avoid blurting out an unguarded retort. He said, more gently: 'There was no real danger, try and forget it. Come over to the fire and have a bite to eat. I'll have a good look at your cuts and bruises before we leave. Narayan and I have something to tell you.'

Had they, indeed! 'Tell her as much as concerns her for now'—she could hear him saying it a few seconds ago. She went towards the fire, remembered and exclaimed jerkily: 'Oh, my clothes and things. . . .'

'Okay, okay, calm down! Did you leave them where you bathed?'

'No. They're just back there. I'll get them. You—you startled me when you yelled like that, and I dropped them,' she lied breathlessly.

He grasped her arm forcibly before she could move. 'Jittery as a chipmunk!' He took her over to the fire and plumped her down on the box Narayan had lately packed. 'I'll get your gear. You wrap yourself around this,' picking up the pan of baked beans and handing it to her with a cloth. 'Careful, it's hot. Here, eat with a spoon, it's easier.'

While he went for her clothes Narayan poured her a mug of hot, black coffee. Then they stood watching her, and she was conscious of the swift glances that passed between them although she kept her head down and forced herself to eat some of the beans. The silence was torture and her heart raced uncomfortably like her thoughts.

What did those glances mean? Finding her clothes so near the camp, had Luke guessed she had been eavesdropping? Narayan was the one who had insisted that the only alternative was to take her with them. But Luke ... Luke had obviously been against it at first, and had had to be reasoned into it. He must have had something else in mind for her. Such as disposing of her quietly? Or leaving her behind in the jungle to fend for herself? Would he change his mind again? Would Narayan be strong enough to prevent him from....

All at once her months of torment, the accident, her fright over the python and larger, nameless fears merged into the quality of a nightmare. Her hand shook so much she couldn't get the spoon to her mouth. Her throat had seized up and she couldn't swallow. The pan slid off her lap and rattled on the ground.

Luke was on his heels beside her. 'Selina?' He smoothed a hand over her hair, cupped and lifted her face to look into her dilated pupils. If she had any thought at all in that numb second, it was the expectation of feeling his powerful hand closing round her throat. Instead, he ran his thumb across her quivering lips. 'You're still in shock, *liefje*! I should have realised. That scare you've had on top of everything else has knocked you sideways.' He drew her into the hollow of his shoulder with gentleness.

Selina stiffened against her drowning senses which were urging her to relax into oblivion on the hard muscles beneath her cheek. She must take hold of herself at all costs and not betray the true reason for being in such a state of panic. 'Leave her to me,' he had told Narayan. He would get her to co-operate. Persuasive tricks like this one, using re-assurance and a soft, deep voice. 'How do you know we're not unscrupulous?'—he had said it himself. And whatever her physical senses were telling her to the contrary, she couldn't trust him.

She sat away from him. Luke picked up the mug of coffee and gave it to her, observing her closely with a frown between his thick golden brows. The enamel mug clattered against her teeth as she tried to take a sip and Luke had to support it for her while she drank the hot, bitter-sweet liquid. When he put it aside she deliberately avoided his shrewd grey eyes, looking to see what had become of the pan of baked beans. Patch had wolfed the lot and was assiduously licking and snuffling around the empty pan.

Luke caught her wrists, albeit gently, and made her face him. 'Listen, Selina, let's get one or two things sorted out now, I think you'll feel better for it. If you're at all harassed by the thought of how you're going to manage on your own getting back to England, your worries are over. You can come with us, and when we've finished the job we're doing we'll see you safe, without interference from Spender or anyone else. It'll be a rough, mountain trek. The going's hard and tiring. You'll have to keep up and keep fit. But we reckon you'll make it. What do you say?'

What did he expect? That she would leap at it ecstatically? Selina removed her wrists from Luke's grasp, one at a time very pointedly.

'That depends.' She was quaking inside but asked coldly: 'What exactly is this job you're doing?'

Luke's expressive brows slanted as though it were a very impertinent question. 'It doesn't concern you. We can't discuss it.'

Anger revived her. 'Why not?' she demanded.

'What you don't know you can't betray, however innocently.' He rose and loomed over her. 'It involves safety, and human lives, Selina.'

'Yours, I suppose,' scornfully. 'And presumably mine, if I agree.'

'Indirectly. But more important other people's. Some of them irredeemable, some of them plain foolish, most of them young and vulnerable like you.'

He was quite serious, and so positive and convincing in the way he spoke that she looked up at him and stammered: 'I d-don't understand....'

'You don't have to, but you'd better believe it. We're wasting time here, Selina. Are you coming or not?'

She was thoroughly bewildered again, forcibly reminded that this man had saved *her* life a couple of times already. How could she have been so muddle-headed as to forget, and imagine that he would harm her? How could she doubt his integrity?

But then she hardly knew him, and he might—he just might turn out to be a plausible rogue. Come to think of it, his enigmatic excuses had made no sense. It sounded like a secret mission out of a preposterous thriller, and her confusion and distrust of his motives lingered.

She tilted her chin and pursed her mouth. 'Do I have a choice?'

'Sure,' he snapped back sardonically. 'Either you

take your chances with us. Or you go back to Henry
Spender.'

'What if I don't choose to do either?'

'Tough luck, Miss Roxley, there are no other
options.'

He looked down at her stubbornly suspicious expression for a moment, then swung towards the
Indian and cast up his brows and hands in exasperation. Narayan shrugged and shook his head. Luke
turned to her and said: 'Okay, have it your own way.
We'll leave you near Kaladhungi and you can make
the best of it until Spender catches up with you.'

'Don't bother.' She threw him a challenging
glance. 'Just give me my jeep and a few directions to
the nearest village.'

Narayan interposed: 'There is no village between
here and Kaladhungi.'

'There must be!' She looked searchingly at Narayan's impassive face, then back to Luke. 'I—I heard
a cock crowing this morning. People keep chickens.
It can't be that far. . . .'

Luke's crack of laughter cut across her. 'Jungle
fowl, you little greenhorn! Don't you know that
domesticated poultry all over the world originated
centuries ago from the tough little Indian jungle
fowl?'

'Oh-h-h!' She felt deflated. Even Narayan had a
ghost of a smile. To cover herself she said with as
much spirit as she could muster: 'I'm not a walking
encyclopaedia like you! All right—as far as Kaladhungi, then.'

'In that case,' amusement still lurked in Luke's
eyes, giving way to a mordant glint as they narrowed
on her, 'we ought to tell you that the situation's

changed. Henry Spender has all your escape routes buttoned up. He's back in Delhi raising the roof about you. He's alerted the police, telegraphed the likeliest stationmasters for miles around. He's put up a hefty reward, Selina. Every local police post and impecunious railway clerk in this area is on the lookout. We can't help you any further now. It's merely a matter of time—a few hours, before they collar you.'

Was this another of his ploys? 'I may be a green-horn, Luke, but I'm not that green! How could you possibly know?' she scoffed.

'How do you think? Not by sending smoke signals, that's for sure.'

Narayan said quietly: 'We have a radio contact, Miss Roxley. It's his business to keep us informed. Luke is telling you the unfortunate truth.'

By radio. Of course. And she was sitting on the contraption at this very moment! She got to her feet as if she had been stung and stood looking at the two men in round-eyed consternation. She had no one to turn to, no refuge, no escape. The weight of her dilemma overwhelmed her ... these two strangers conspiring to get to some secret destination, who might implicate her in serious trouble before they discarded her; or Henry and Delia, waiting to pounce on their quarry, who would penalise her mercilessly for the inconvenience and unwelcome publicity she had caused.

Luke was easing her back on the box. The clasp of his hand on her shoulder, the latent strength in every sinew as he bent towards her, seemed to empty her mind. His clear grey eyes held hers until the tension seeped out of her. It was as though he had put a protective wall around her.

'Which is it to be, Selina?' he asked softly.

'I'll go.' Her voice was barely audible.

'To Kaladhungi or with us?'

'With you.' She broke from his gaze and yielded with a sigh.

CHAPTER FOUR

SELINA was full of carefully concealed excitement as she sat beside Luke van Meer in the heavily laden small car again. Pleasurable excitement. Incredible as it seemed after the ordeals of the morning, her mind refused to consider the rights and wrongs of this mysterious expedition any further, preferring to dwell on the possibilities it held. Escape at long last into the Himalayan backwoods, with the wonders of the biggest and most beautiful mountains, the freedom to express herself, the spice of adventure!

And being with Luke. *Wanting* to be with Luke. Inexplicable after only a few hours! except for the fact that he was the antithesis of Henry. From Henry she always knew what to expect; the tyranny of continuous pressure to break her will, and a menacing urbanity that made her spirit shrink. But Luke goaded and aroused her with fluctuating moods, rough one moment, gentle the next, rude, protective, ironic, impersonal. She recognised with astonishment that she could openly defy Luke, yell at him and let herself go, yet turn to him in need as if she had known him all her life. What a paradox that the 'security' Henry had tried to force on her terrified her, while the precarious situation she found herself in with Luke van Meer gave her a cockeyed feeling of exhilaration! She was always scared with Henry and Delia. Suddenly she was no longer scared of Luke and Narayan.

Luke had opened another tin of baked beans before they left camp, and this time she had relished her 'breakfast' straight out of the tin. Luke had squatted beside her and dressed the cuts and bruises on her arms and legs, then tilted her face up and pressed lightly around her eye. It was enough to make her wince and remember the bruised swelling.

'You look like a clown this morning.' His eyes had been mocking. 'Red patches of sunburn and a ring round your eye like a ripening plum.'

Incensed by his unfeeling humour a tart reply had been on the tip of her tongue when it struck her that he was probably right; she hadn't bothered to look at herself in the mirror of her compact or apply any make-up. She glared back at him haughtily instead, but a smile had begun to pull irresistibly at the corners of her mouth.

'Let it go, Selina,' he laughed outright. 'A smile doesn't hurt much. Sorry, we can't do anything about your black eye; it'll fade. But you must have brought some sort of feminine junk to soothe sunburn?'

Feminine junk, indeed! 'I've got some moisturising cream and a bottle of sun-tan oil in my case. What are you doing?' she had asked sharply, and unnecessarily, because he had flicked open the locks on her case and was rummaging through it already, mixing up the contents untidily.

'Here, slap some of that on,' he had tossed her the plastic bottle of expensive sun-tan oil, clipped the case shut and turned away to pack his first-aid box. Everything precisely in its place for *this* box, she thought with a little grimace.

She had spread the sun-tan oil gingerly over her sore skin, then sat and watched, with an almost dazed acceptance, as he and Narayan cleared up the camp, doused the fire and topped up the tanks from petrol cans. She had to get up so that Luke could load the radio equipment, and she followed the husky, broad-shouldered figure to the car.

'I'll—I'll drive the jeep, shall I?' she had suggested tentatively.

'Not a chance! The car for you, Miss Roxley.' He was busy tightening the rope Narayan had thrown to him across the roof rack. 'We can't have you zipping off on another unorthodox joy-ride as soon as we hit the main track.'

'But I wouldn't!' Indignation had made her shrill. 'I only offered because I thought I should help out with the driving.'

'Okay, I'll take your word for it. But there are other reasons. In the jeep you would be a sitting duck for Spender's spotters, if we met anyone. In the car you'll be sheltered from the sun and less conspicuous.' From his old duffle bag he took a rumpled cotton shirt and tore off a sizable strip of it. 'Tie this over your head to hide your hair.'

'I have a perfectly good silk scarf of my own.' Her lip had curled in distaste until she saw his amusement as he said:

'And perfectly recognisable as belonging to Selina Roxley, right? This bit of rag is not very elegant but it's clean—and anonymous. Have you a pair of sun-glasses? Fine. Put them on too, to protect your eye.'

She had done as she was told, stifling the unfamiliar but stimulating feeling that she was at liberty to argue her head off now whenever she chose. Even if she never won an argument with Luke! She had never dared risk an open dispute with Henry and Delia, taking refuge in a doggedly unco-operative silence or icy disdain. It was a heady feeling, being able to yell back if she wanted to, to let it rip sometimes.

And here she was, sitting obediently in the car once more with Luke van Meer, her hair hidden beneath a piece of his shirt knotted under her chin, bumping along an old, timber cart-track through dense forests into open vistas of scrub and grass and back into dark green, lofty trees freckled with sun-light. Narayan had set off ten minutes ahead of them as a precaution, and it was as if they were cut off from the rest of the world.

Unlike the previous day, when she had slept ex-haustedly, Selina felt alert, responding to the rich colours and abundant life of the jungle around them. Sensing her awareness and excitement, Luke gave her an indulgent glance and slowed down from time to time to point things out and answer her questions good-humouredly.

Those trees spreading a haze of deep scarlet blos-soms were called Flame of the Forest, he told her. The tough lianes with mauve flowers were bauhinia. And that other splash of brilliant colour was called *dhak*. 'Dark?' Selina rolled the sound of it happily on her tongue. 'Anything but!' for the flowers had bright orange-red petals contrasting with velvety black calyxes. As the sun climbed, an odour of hot, earthy green vegetation hung on the air.

She had a glimpse of wild pig rooting in the undergrowth; and in an open glade, resting in the camouflage of dappled shade, a herd of chital which leapt up and took off in alarm on the approach of the car, reminding her, with swift intake of breath, of the previous day's accident. A little farther on she saw a handsome young sambur buck, his antlers much larger and more imposing than the chital. The sambur belled a warning call and vanished, his dun brown colour merging into the jungle.

'A tasty bit of venison for Sher Bahadur,' Luke said. Selina had removed her sun-glasses for a better view and with another glance at her engrossed expression and the enquiry in her large, violet eyes, he added: 'The lordly tiger.'

'Do you think,' she clasped her hands together as a little frisson of trepidation ran over her skin, 'we'll see one? Back home they're in zoos and safari parks, and I saw some in a circus once when I was a child; poor old captive creatures roaring and doing tricks when the whip cracked. But it wouldn't be the same, here in the jungle where they truly belong.'

'I doubt if we'll be so lucky, Selina. It's an endangered species. Very few of them left in the wild. Fortunately they are protected now and a few dedicated spirits are trying to reverse the trend. Maybe those zoos and safari parks will be able to help out by rearing strong young tiger cubs to be brought back here where they belong. Then nature can gradually take over again and build up the numbers by breeding. A long, tricky job of conservation, but well worth the effort.'

'Oh, yes!' she agreed fervently. 'And we can help by contributing money to wildlife schemes. I would ... if I could. ...' her voice died.

There was silence between them until a troop of

monkeys, intent on crossing the track, scrambled through the trees chittering with rage at the car, then swung away into denser cover. They looked familiar to Selina and Luke said: 'They're rhesus monkeys, used for research in the West. The ubiquitous *bandar* of the plains and foothills. You'll see a lot more of those.'

But the high spot of the journey for Selina came when she heard a shrill cackling sound like a frisky farmyard bantam. She turned to Luke with an excited little cry. 'Over there,' he grinned, 'in those thickets. Look quick or you'll miss them.' He slowed to a crawl.

The jungle fowl had scattered, but she caught the flash of a perky crest of comb and glossy feathers resembling a black-breasted red game cock, and laughed with unashamed delight not only at her own mistake that morning but in the sheer joy of discovery. As she craned through the window, hoping for another last glimpse, Luke's mocking grin altered subtly, softening to a new light in his eyes before he laughed too.

'Chanticleer!' She slid on her glasses again. 'Straight out of a fairy tale. He was sweet!'

'You wouldn't think so if you'd seen the fiendish spurs they have like extra talons at the back above the claws. Lethal in a cockfight,' he said dryly. '*Nature, red in tooth and claw*, as Tennyson once put it. But it's all part of a magnificently complex cycle of inter-dependence which enriches our world. Until mankind comes along and upsets the balance of nature for his own greedy ends.'

'I suppose it's impossible to protect wildlife completely from *human* predators!' she sighed, 'but I know how you feel.'

Shadowy forest gave place to dazzling sunshine across miles of rambling scrub jungle. The silence was suddenly oppressive. Selina threw him a side-long look, wondering nervously what she could possibly have said to offend him. She saw his knuckles taut on the wheel, as though he was hold-ing anger down or would have liked to be able to grip somebody by the throat. His preoccupation lasted a full minute, then:

'I feel even more strongly about protecting human lives from the greedy two-legged predators who prey on them!' he said savagely. 'Man's vicious in-humanity to man.' He put his foot down hard on the accelerator.

Disconcerted, she couldn't think of anything to say. Something about the tone of this terse, scorch-ing denunciation told her he was not generalising. Who, in particular, was he thinking of? Could he be referring to Henry's behaviour?—was that why he had consented to bring her with them in spite of the risks? She rubbed her fingers along the be-wildered lines of her forehead. Of course not. Luke didn't know enough about her individual circum-stances to provoke such fierce condemnation; and protecting human lives was too grand an aspiration to apply to one insignificant girl he had met only the day before.

Then what was he talking about? Whose 'in-humanity' had caught him on the raw and turned him into an implacable adversary? Whatever the injustice was, it had outraged Luke so deeply that it had become almost a personal vendetta. She under-

stood this as intuitively as she knew now that his
obsession was somehow bound up with the trek they
were on. Perhaps even the main reason for it, going
by what he had said earlier today.

But what on earth was there to fight for in the
remote reaches of the Himalayas? What could this
secret objective be? One look at his forbidding pro-
file was sufficient to crush the question she longed
to ask. Presently she saw his hands relax on the
wheel, and the tenseness went out of her too, but
his moods were too unpredictable for her to pursue
the conversation. The perplexities crowding her
mind remained unspoken.

The stalwart little car bounced along a narrow
trail through a stretch of tall, billowing elephant
grass and eventually came out on to a rutted road
where Luke put on speed, presumably to make up
for the time lost dawdling through the forests. A
lorry went past going the other way and Selina
shrank down in the seat, instantly conscious of the
fact that they were back in a world of other people,
however sparsely populated it might be, and that
the problem of disguising her identity would soon
have to be faced. Strange that Luke hadn't mentioned Narayan's suggestions about it so far, she
thought, coughing in the thin swirl of white dust
the lorry had left behind which was blowing across
her side of the car.

'Another few miles of rough riding and we'll take
a break.' Luke flicked her one of his amused glances.
'A bit of dust on the sun-tan oil will do wonders for
your complexion.'

What else could she expect from the unfeeling
brute! she thought crossly, fumbling for a hand-

kerchief. He reached forward and pulled a man-sized tissue from the jumble under the dashboard, and she wiped her nose and mouth and the grit from her tongue, thankful that the sun-glasses had shielded her eyes. In the distance there were two figures near the roadside and as they drew nearer Selina saw that they were village women in off-white wrap-around garments more like sheets than the gracefully draped *saris* sophisticated Indian women wore. They were padding along in single file, the one in front with a basket on her head, the one behind leading a cow.

The speedometer needle swung back; Luke tooted the horn sharply. A moment later, to Selina's amazement, both women scuttled across the road in front of the car like startled rabbits, leaving the cow behind. As the car went past Luke saluted them with a grin, at which they immediately pulled their head-cloths bashfully across their faces.

'Just as well you slowed down!' Selina scolded in her haughtiest tone. 'They must have been scared out of their wits by the horn. Dashing over the road in that stupid way at the last minute! I suppose they're not used to seeing much traffic along here, poor things.'

'You have a lot to learn, Miss Supercilious Roxley!' His grey eyes were dancing with amusement. 'They may be villagers—yokels to you—but they're far from stupid. You had to take the brunt of the lorry's dust a mile back. They avoided ours. When they heard the horn they looked to see which way the wind was blowing and crossed over. As soon as the dust settles they'll be moving on.'

She subsided in the seat and said, 'Oh-h-h,' in a small voice.

'Cheer up,' he spoke briskly. 'At least you were concerned about them, your heart's in the right place.'

'So were you, concerned I mean—slowing down and warning them.'

'Sure. My heart's in the right place too.' The hint of mockery was back as he caught her hand and held it to his side. 'Here, feel.'

The warmth of his body and the steady heartbeat against her hand sent a sharp rush of feeling through her. She bit her lip and jerked her hand from his clasp. The quizzical tilt of his brow in her direction brought a wave of painful colour to the tender burn on her cheeks, and she assured herself that it was the way his mood kept changing that was the cause of her discomfiture. Her own moods seemed to veer perilously with his.

'It was meant as a joke, so don't get any uppity ideas,' he said with a touch of impatience. 'Trying to get you to smile is like cracking a safe, and I have yet to hear you laugh, really laugh without inhibitions, though that cockerel back there in the jungle came near to achieving it. It was a good sound, you ought to try it more often.'

'I haven't much of a sense of humour,' she turned her face away to the window, 'that's what you're saying, isn't it?'

'Okay, don't take umbrage.' He paused, then said on a softer, gentler note: 'I guess you haven't had much to laugh at lately.'

'No....' She didn't want to think about Henry and Delia. She could still feel the warmth and the

strong, regular heartbeat on the back of her hand,
unconsciously rubbing it with her other palm as
if to wipe it away. She hadn't enjoyed the release of
free, unrestrained laughter for a long, long time;
and if Luke found the repressions forced on her
amusing, he could laugh his head off at her for all
she cared!

He said reflectively: 'Exactly how old are you,
Selina?'

'I'll be eighteen in a month's time,' she informed
him woodenly.

'Oh, my God! Under age! I never gave it a
thought because you look older. Old enough——'

'For what?' she interjected sharply, a sudden
catch in her breath.

'To make your own decisions. Yesterday it looked
like a fair gamble, assisting a young woman in a tight
corner. Now it turns out we're harbouring a runaway minor against the wishes of her guardians. Or
worse! Abduction—kidnapping—you name it, they
could charge us with it after this little caper! Why
didn't you tell me you're under age?'

'Why didn't you ask me?' She covered a sudden
pang of anxiety with indignation. 'You're the know-
all who checked in my passport for everything else.'
The anxiety was gathering into a knot inside her.

'So I glanced at the birth date, but who had the
time to reckon it by a few months one way or the
other? You were knocked out and dead beat, remember? And woman-shaped in all the right places.'

'Wel-ll! Thank you for those few kind words!'

'Cool it, Selina. It's too late to make any difference
now. First things first. We'll have to pull a few

strings and get all the complications sorted out afterwards.'

A wave of relief washed over her and she pressed
the back of her wrist to the moisture which had
broken out on her forehead and upper lip. Exactly
what she had been expecting him to do on discover-
ing she was a minor wasn't clear, but it had ripped
away some of the shaky confidence she had been
building up.

He said grimly: 'Spender will have to answer for
a good deal himself. Inveigling a young girl into
going to an isolated place and scaring the hell out
of her. Maybe he could have got away with it at
that. What's the age of consent in England, about
sixteen? Of all the crazy anomalies! Legally you're
not a responsible adult, yet old enough to be seduced
if you can be persuaded or pressured into consent-
ing.'

'He did put on the pressure ... they both did. I
had to fight to stop— stop him ... you know what I
mean,' she faltered. 'Oh, he ... he wanted me all
right, but he had other motives as well.'

'Consent is one thing, coercion is rape, he knows
that.' Luke scanned her face and the bitter line
of her mouth, then down to the slender white hands
clasping and unclasping restlessly in her lap. One
big square hand closed over hers stilling the restless-
ness. His grip was brief, hard and sympathetic, and
her heart swelled with emotion.

'I'll never go back to them ... never, whatever
the consequences! I'll kill myself first!' she cried
from the depths of overwrought feelings.

'Be quiet!' he rapped out in such a harsh voice
that Selina threw up her head and stared at him.

His face was contorted, his grey glance almost black with a kind of rage. 'Do you know what you're saying, you impetuous little fool? If I hear you dramatising yourself again about suicide, if I even suspect you're thinking that way, I'll tan your bottom!'

Selina squeezed back against her door, holding her breath. She had had wild thoughts about it once or twice in the last few months when hysteria threatened to overpower her, but how much she had intended it was another matter. She was too spirited to accept defeat. She couldn't think why she had blurted out such a silly statement, except to convince him of her determination to get away from Henry and Delia, whether she was under age or not.

'Luke,' she pleaded in a wobbly voice, 'I didn't mean it. It was just ... just a figure of speech. But I meant what I said about not going back.'

After a moment he gave her a smile of such friendly warmth that she let out her breath in a long sigh.

'Okay,' he said. 'I told you before, Narayan and I will see you safe when this is all over.'

'You won't hand me over,' she pressed urgently, 'whatever happens?'

'I guarantee you that.' His voice was clipped, but the assertion held an unequivocal promise, and Selina leaned her head against the seat and shut her eyes, the worried lines gradually smoothing out of her thin, patrician features.

But her eyelids flew open again before many minutes had passed, for the car had left the road and was jolting along another timber track which cut through a sal forest and petered out on the bank of a canal. On the far side of the canal was the

brown, green and yellow patchwork of fields and
paths, a remote grove of dark-leaved mango trees
and, beyond that, half-hidden walls and roofs, probably the village to which the two women had been
making their way.

The sun was high and hot, the small car had
begun to warm up like an oven. Selina sat forward
and felt the cotton kaftan clinging to the sweat on
her back. Luke pulled up in the shade of a large
flowering tree and when he had shifted his big,
muscular body out of the confined space she realised
just how much heat the controlled vitality of the
man could generate. She was suddenly more aware
of his explicit masculinity than at any moment since
she had seen him coming back from the river the
night before. She couldn't take her eyes off him as
he walked round the bonnet.

'Want a drink?' Luke opened her door allowing
a comparatively cool draught of air through the car.
'Lime juice and water?' She nodded, twisting her
head away. He must have mistaken the constraint
in her manner for sulky dissatisfaction at the dis-
comforts she was putting up with, and added with
drawling satire: 'My apologies, Your Highness, for
not being able to offer you an air-conditioned limousine and iced champagne.'

She had to get away from him, if only for a few
minutes. She slid out of the car, carefully avoiding
any physical contact with him, and went off towards
the darker line of trees calling, 'Back in a minute'
over her shoulder. The gloom of the forest put a
stop to her ludicrous flight. She stood in the middle
of a small glade, with her hand pressed to her lips,
listening intently, but if there was any movement

in the jungle the sound was drowned by the thud-
ding of her heart.

She had been too worked up and weary in the last
twenty-four hours to consider Luke's emphatic
virility. A dynamic man. Not handsome, but blunt
and physically powerful, with a blatant, assertive
masculinity that was bound to attract him to women.
Herself included. But this was too alarming a notion
to dwell on. She was bogged down in enough problems and confusions already without jeopardising
her peace of mind still further with misgivings of
this kind about Luke van Meer.

Five minutes on her own was enough to pull herself together. Selina tidied her jeans and kaftan, re-
tied the rag on her head and sauntered back to the
canal. Luke had been leaning against the car,
smoking. She looked him straight in the eye, determinedly casual, and settled herself in the front seat
again, taking out her compact and the sun-tan oil
and spreading another layer of it on her skin. Her
black eye was less swollen but a rich, fruity hue. No
man would give her a second glance, not even Luke
van Meer, while she looked as battered and scruffy
as this! she thought wryly. And in her present
circumstances it was just as well.

Luke had pushed away from the car and gone
round to the boot. He came back with some lime
juice for her, scrutinising her with judicious thor-
oughness before passing her the mug. She put on
her sun-glasses, tossed her handbag on to the other
seat and took a sip of the cool, tangy liquid. She
said nonchalantly: 'It's sultry today, isn't it.'

'Yep.' There was a faint smile on his mouth as he
sat down in the shadow of the car, stretched out his

long legs and propped his back against the door near her feet. She drank the lime juice slowly and gazed around at the canal, the distant village, the trees, anything but Luke, wishing she could think of something more to say, wishing she still wasn't so acutely conscious of his robust maleness as he sprawled within reach of her hand.

She flickered a glance down at him. His eyes were closed. She let her glance drift over him for a stolen second. He had unbuttoned his loose, ill-fitting bush shirt and pushed it aside to let what little breeze there was get to his smooth, sun-browned skin, and Selina could see the mass of golden hair on dark tan diminishing in a fleecy line to the taut, flat muscles of his stomach. The gold-spiked lashes against his broad cheekbones moved and opened slightly. She shifted her eyes instantly, but not soon enough to escape a glimmer of steely grey which made her nerves jump.

Staring with assumed concentration at the thick, waxy blossoms of the tree under which they were parked, she said in what she hoped was a steady, composed voice: 'It's a magnificent tree, Luke, what is it?'

'Um-m-m?' he tipped his head back to look at it. '*Semul* ... silk cotton.'

'I thought cotton grew on bushes.' She was prattling. 'And silkworms lived on mulberry trees.' Of all the inane remarks! she thought.

'Neither of those,' he replied lazily. 'This one grows a large seedpod full of silky cotton floss. Very useful, but it can't be spun in the ordinary way. Heard of kapok? That's the stuff. They used to put it in mattresses and cushions, lifebelts, sleeping bags too. It doesn't absorb water, so it's good for keeping the warmth in and the wet out.' He relaxed and shut his eyes. 'Are you hungry?'

Lethargy invaded her limbs. 'Not particularly. It's too hot.'

'We'll take another ten minutes before moving on.'

When they returned to the main road and resumed their journey Selina found that a short, uneasy doze had done nothing to dispel her disquiet. She knew little about Luke's real motives, nor his intentions towards her. Still less, now, about her own capacity to resist him. He was no Henry: physically she wouldn't stand a chance against him. As a friend and ally he would be all that she could have hoped for; but if he chose to exert himself in other ways....

With Luke filling the little car with his forceful presence so close beside her, she wondered how she could have been so ingenuously happy and frank with him all morning. The result was that the constraint between them developed into an edgy, almost pulsating silence, and after a few miles of this Luke turned a swift, scowling glance on her, then glowered over the wheel and said bitingly:

'God knows what you're so uptight about all of a sudden, Miss Roxley, but if you've decided in the last half hour—with typically feminine perversity —that you don't like the conditions out here, let me remind you that you let yourself in for this when you first absconded with the jeep. A sullen temper won't improve matters. Try and come to terms with it.'

'I've ... I've got a headache,' she retorted mor-

osely, a panicky evasion which was speedily coming
true. And it was no consolation to have his manner
alter at once to gentler concern as he said:

'I'll give you something for that, and you can
rest as soon as we make camp.'

Narayan was waiting for them in the shelter of
a dry watercourse near a hilly track. Selina couldn't
wait to get out, and as she stood flexing the slightly
stiff muscles of her graceful arms and legs, the ex-
uberant pi-dog came scampering across the scree
to hurl himself at her, barking and leaping a welcome that would have warmed a sterner heart. She
laughed shakily, blinking back absurd tears as she
fended him off and petted him.

She heard Luke say: 'I guess since he sniffed you
out of the elephant grass like a pedigree bloodhound
he reckons you belong to him. I've never seen him
take to anyone so quickly.' And looking round she
realised that he and Narayan had been watching the
boisterous pantomime with amusement.

She straightened defensively. 'I've never owned
a dog. But I like him.'

'Well, don't get too fond of the flea-bitten scallywag.'

Luke's blunt, offhand tone brought her down to
earth, reminding her again of her insecurity in this
venture. 'I won't,' she returned loftily, and moved
away from the two men, deliberately isolating herself as they started to set up the camp.

By this time her head was well and truly aching
with physical and psychological fatigue. She scrambled through a wash, without changing her clothes,
pecked uninterestedly at a stew Luke had recon-
stituted from a camping pack, swallowed the pills

he gave her and rolled herself up in a blanket co-coon, turning her back on the flickering fire with a shiver. In these sub-montane valleys the temperature dropped drastically at night.

She knew the men had taken the radio equipment away, further down the stony ravine, and there were no comforting voices, only the whirring of cicadas and an occasional nightjar. It had been a strange day of turmoil and unpredictable emotions, and she was no nearer finding out what was going on, or what lay ahead of her.

The pills began to work, the tensions and headache faded. She slept.

CHAPTER FIVE

LUKE's advice about coming to terms with herself and with the extraordinary events which had befallen her must have penetrated Selina's subconscious, for when she woke the next morning, after a good twelve hours of deep, undisturbed sleep, she felt stronger physically and quite calm and cheerful. She stretched and a new, tingling vibrance ran along her muscles as her brain took stock of the situation.

She had passed a turning point in her life and would have to accept what was happening to her. There was no reason in the world why she shouldn't adjust to her changed circumstances and get as much enjoyment out of them as she could—while she could.

What was it called? ... the Eastern concept of destiny? She fumbled over the side of the cot for her shoes and banged them out on the stony ground before swinging her feet down to put them on. *Kismet!* ... the word for fate. There had been an inevitability about the way things had worked out: her decision to escape from the rest-house coinciding with the arrival of Luke and Narayan in the reserve, the singular chance that brought them to her rescue and the unforeseen developments which had pitchforked her into joining Luke's mysterious crusade into the mountains. *Kismet.*

As for Luke himself.... She dismantled the mosquito net, and carefully folded and rolled up the blanket as she mulled it over. In all Luke's dealings with her so far, whether harsh or friendly or ironically flippant, there had been nothing even vaguely suggestive, no attempt at making a pass, nothing to provoke *that* sort of apprehension in her. Her own awareness had welled up, unbidden, in her own mind.

It was all Henry's fault, she thought waspishly, running her fingers through her sleep-tousled hair. He had distorted her ideas about men and the relationships between men and women to the point where she was terrified of getting the slightest bit involved with anyone again. She would have to make a real mental effort and put it into perspective. School herself to behave naturally. Starting with Luke now, and later with other men she would be meeting in the normal course of life. This was going to be part of her new freedom, learning to handle human relationships in a balanced, self-possessed way.

Flinging open the tent flap, she breezed out, humming a little tune, to find that the camp had been cleared up except for her tent and the remains of the camp fire. The sun was fairly high already, Narayan had gone, taking Patch with him. She could see Luke bending over the bonnet of the car, tinkering with the engine.

'Oh, Luke!' she wailed guiltily. 'I overslept. Why didn't you wake me?'

He strolled over, wiping his hands on a piece of rag. 'Since I gave you something last night to put you out like a light,' he grinned, 'I had to give you time to sleep it off. Beans do you for breakfast again, or are you sick of them?'

'Yes, of course they'll do,' she said agitatedly. 'I'll just have a wash and tidy myself up.' She picked up a water bottle and scrambled across the dry river bed into the bushes. Luke seemed in a good humour, prepared to overlook her tetchy behaviour the day before. Thank goodness he had assumed that she was off-colour! although it was rather disturbing to think he could give her something that would knock her out so effectively. No time to fuss about that, at the moment. No harm had come to her and she felt good.

The amicable mood lasted all morning between them, over mugs of coffee and tins of beans, packing up the remnants and setting out on the dusty scree surface of the old watercourse. A flock of gaudy green parakeets screeched across overhead as they reached the main road. Thereafter conversation was limited, but the silences were natural and unstrained.

Selina was excited when at last they left the jungle for the mountains. They turned on to a cart track which went up a slow gradient through dense patches of clerodendron massed with spiky whorls of blossom, then across a grassy ridge and on between shimmering green terraces of cultivation which descended like the neat flounces of a skirt around a shallow hill. Cattle huts appeared, then small, simple, mud-and-lime washed houses built round muddy courtyards. Soon the car was coasting down a gentle slope flanked on either side by a little row of open booths.

The bazaar, if it was big enough to be called that, had been dormant in the brilliant sun, but when the car arrived a swarm of barefooted brown children came tumbling out. Luke braked under a gnarled tree with large exposed roots which clung precariously to the stony, crumbling roadside. The children began clambering around the car, white teeth flashing in broad smiles on their brown faces. The shopkeepers stepped down from their booths to join in the welcome while their womenfolk stood on the outskirts shyly hiding their faces, their eyes bright with curiosity as they stared over the corners of their headcloths.

With her spirits soaring now, and intent on making the most of any opportunity to explore, Selina asked eagerly: 'May I get out, Luke?' He ignored her, leaning from the window to call one of the men.

'Please, Luke?' she persisted. 'Only for a minute to look around?'

'Okay, but it won't take me long to find out where Narayan has gone to pick a site for us, so don't go wandering off.'

She pushed the car door open, swung her feet out and stood up, smiling at the cluster of children. Running a hand under her improvised headscarf, she lifted the sweat-damp tendrils of silky chestnut hair off her neck and felt a slight chill on her skin. Although the village was in the lower foothills, scarcely a thousand feet above the jungle valleys, the air here was distinctly cooler and she took deep breaths of it before strolling back towards the bazaar.

Escorted by the troop of giggling children, she peered into the small, square booths, sniffing at the musty smell of gunny sacks full of rice and millet and chick-pea *gram*, and the more pungent odours of garlic, cloves and ginger roots. She was fascinated with the colourful pyramids of curry spices and glossy green and red chillies, the crystalline chunks of salt, the rough brown lumps of *jaggery* which she had been told was sweet stuff made from sugar palm sap. One booth was festooned with gaily coloured little packets of tea strung together and flapping in the breeze like miniature flags; another tinkled with the sound of a myriad glass and silver bangles and other trinkets.

She stopped for a moment to watch a portly shopkeeper weighing dark, stone-milled flour on an old-fashioned balance which he held dangling from his fat brown fingers in front of a wizened crone. They had an argument, the woman spread part of her head-shawl and he tipped the flour into it as though it were a shopping bag. A coin changed hands and as the crone moved slowly away, still muttering to herself, Selina felt a surge of compassion for the tiny, stooped figure with wispy white hair, arms like matchsticks and scarred bare feet, but there was nothing she could do to help.

She was standing looking into another stall, speculating on what some moist, brownish-black balls on a big brass tray could possibly be, when a pair of hands came down lightly on her shoulders. She turned to look up into Luke's face. Sunlight caught the lighter strands of his thick, roughly cut hair, streaking it with gold, and put a golden sheen on his tanned skin along the line of his jaw, mouth and chin. For a moment or two she gazed at the firm outline of his lips and wanted to reach up and touch them. She saw the corners lift in a mocking smile and her gaze flew up to the glint in his eyes. His brows rose questioningly.

Selina looked hastily away to the stall and said: 'Luke, what—what's that beastly brownish stuff? Do they eat it?' She hoped her voice sounded steadier than she felt.

'Tobacco.' There was an underlying tinge of laughter.

Was he laughing because she had been staring in a bemused way?—how could he tell, anyway, behind the lenses of her sun-glasses? He always found her ignorance comical. That was all it was. And it infuriated her.

'You're pulling my leg,' she said shortly.

'Miss Roxley, I wouldn't dare,' he drawled mockingly, then proceeded to enlighten her in a matter-of-fact tone. 'They burn a piece of that in a small, shallow terra-cotta bowl with a hollow stem which they hold in a special way cupped between their palms so that they can suck in the smoke.' His hands slid over her shoulders and closed round her upper arms. 'Back to the car now.'

As he swung her about-face and nudged her forward she eyed a display of golden brown squirls in syrup and other exotic Indian confections on which bees and flies were crawling torpidly. She wrinkled her nose in distaste, but one of the children, bolder than the rest, called out something and the little brown faces grinned at them hopefully. It was the universal language of appeal. Selina glanced at Luke, but he shook his head.

'No buying sweets for them, or giving them money. You've aroused enough curiosity already.' Then, seeing the look on her face, he added gruffly as he urged her into the car: 'I'll fix a tip for the headman of the village. He can buy them sweets when we're well out of the way.'

Beyond the village the rutted cart-track forked and Luke took the more substantial road winding down heavily wooded slopes on the dark side of the hill until they were within sight of a much bigger river valley than the one they had used the first night. Turning off on a watering trail for cattle brought them out on to a broad bank of scree and rocky shale by the river. A spiral of smoke in the distance showed where Narayan already had a camp fire going. Luke drove along the bank and parked beside the jeep.

Selina slid eagerly out of the passenger seat, but as she acknowledged Patch's vociferous welcome the chill air struck through her thin shortie kaftan again, and it occurred to her, for the first time, that the higher they went into the mountains the colder it was going to be, and she was hardly equipped for raw March winds in the Himalayas.

She was worriedly rubbing some warmth into the goose-bumps on her arms when Luke said sharply: 'Are you cold? Even in the sun?'

'It's nothing. I'll move around and be all right in a minute.'

'For a runaway going back to the English climate you didn't pack much sensible clothing, did you?' was the sarcastic comment. 'Imprudent as ever!'

'I put in the woolly sweater and slacks I wore on the plane coming out, but in the panic I left my fur coat in the rest-house. I thought I'd buy something in Delhi to replace it.' Then acidly: 'I wasn't planning a trek.'

'Well, don't get snappish. We'll find a remedy for that.' He fetched her his old cardigan from the car.

'Put that on for now.'

Although huge for her the cardigan banished the chills. She had a jab of anxiety about his 'remedy'. Abandon her, or send her back to the plains? He couldn't do that ... not after his promise. The baggy grey knitwear hung on her almost to the knees, but who cared? Stifling a giggle, she rolled back the sleeves. When Narayan and Luke began to talk in confidential undertones she moved apart from them to look at the view.

About half a mile upstream the river poured through a gorge of towering, perpendicular slabs of bare sandstone and foamed over large boulders worn smooth by the roaring torrent. Then it levelled into a wide, open run of scree, shallows and rock-strewn pools on its way out of the foothills. The clear, pure air from the mountains whirled down the thickly forested ravines at the head of the valley, soughed through the trees along the river and flirted the leaves over in dancing light, and every now and then a strong gust swept up a mist of spray that stung her skin with tiny droplets.

Selina drew a deep breath, spread her arms wide as if to embrace the whole alien splendour of this Himalayan scene, and sighed with satisfaction. In spite of her bruises and tribulations she felt strong and healthy and marvellously alive. She was suddenly very hungry, with a sharp edge of restored appetite.

She went back to the camp fire. While Narayan settled down to eat some Indian curry which he must have purchased in the village, Luke and she ate hard-boiled eggs with flat, round, wholemeal pancakes called *chupatties* liberally spread with a spicy chutney. It was reminiscent of some impromptu dinners of her childhood when she had surreptitiously raided the larder and taken anything she could find, but she thoroughly enjoyed it. She also helped herself to a chunk of sweet, dark red, guava 'cheese' from a tin, and licked the delicious flavour off her fingers. This was followed by the ripest, speckled yellow fruit from the hand of bananas the two men had brought with them, and mugs of good, strong, sweet tea.

Replete, and conscious of a growing sense of physical well-being, Selina jumped up and began to collect the mugs and other oddments they had used, intending to take them down to the river to wash. Luke leaned back against the bole of the tree and at the click of his lighter she looked round and met his glinting gaze, the sunlight picking up creases of amusement about his mouth and eyes as he removed the cigarette and blew a feather of smoke.

'What's so funny now?' she demanded imperiously.

'You are.' She threw up her head, challenging him to explain by the disdainful tilt of her chin. He said: 'If your classy friends could see you now, Miss Roxley, they would cut you out of the smart set without compunction. A black eye, scruffy garments and a rag round your head. Stuffing your pretty mouth with coarse bread and bananas as if you haven't eaten for a week. Tch, tch!' he clicked his tongue in mock disapproval.

Colour invaded her face. 'Well, I was hungry.' Ugly memories came back. Recovering, she said acidly: 'It's *your* old cardigan! What did you expect? A dreamy luncheon gown with a picture hat and parasol? Where have you been all this time, or haven't you seen ordinary girls out on a hike or a picnic?'

'You an ordinary working girl?' his brow quirked mockingly.

She faltered a second. 'How do you know I'm not?'

'Look at your hands, Selina—your graceful, unsullied hands. Your clothes have taken a beating, but they came out of the top drawer. The way you talk, the way you move, the way you look down your patrician nose at lesser mortals.' He grinned outright. 'In your own elegant circle I suspect you're a snob, Miss Roxley.'

'Little you know!' she retorted bitterly. 'Anyway, must you be rude?'

'You're confusing rudeness with honesty.'

'And you're confusing honesty with—with prejudice. You've written me off as rich, pampered and good for nothing from the moment we met. Nothing I could say or do would shake it out of your bigoted head!'

'Rich, yes, and spoilt in the way of creature comforts,' he affirmed, still grinning maddeningly, 'in spite of a few other hardships.'

The remembrance of all her suffering choked her with burning indignation. 'You think money makes up for everything? You and your superficial judgements! You're like everyone else at home who wouldn't accept the truth.'

'Atta girl!' He shouted with laughter, an infectious sound accompanied by a mime of putting up his fists, jabbing and parrying in a mock sparring match. Narayan began to chuckle quietly and the

dog yapped and danced round Selina, agitated by
the raised voices.

Her indignation died away, but she quelled a
strong inclination to join in the laughter, fluttering
her long lashes down on her cheeks and saying in
a fiercely contemptuous tone: 'I pity your wife—if
any woman's been witless enough to marry you!
You're so boorish and obtuse, and so pigheaded
about your own pet theories and interests, that the
poor wretch probably has to put up with as miserable
an existence as I've had!'

'If you're fishing to find out if I'm married, come
right out and ask. I'm not—at the moment.' His
eyes narrowed wickedly. 'Since you're inured to
hardship and we have no illusions about each other,
how about taking me on, Miss Roxley?'

She suddenly recalled Narayan's suggestion that
Luke should pass her off as his wife. Her eyes
opened, large and round, the colour of the irises
darkened. Idiotic of her to have used that silly jibe!
She wanted to retaliate but managed to curb the
incautious reply that sprang to her lips and
breathed frustratedly: 'I'm not standing here talking nonsense any more!' And swinging round, she
stalked off towards the river with the mugs and
utensils clanking noisily as she went.

Squatting on her haunches and swilling the utensils vigorously in a swirl of water at the river's edge,
she looked down at her hands. One of her nails had
broken, and there were scratches here and there, but
Luke was right. They were not working hands. She
would learn, and do her share around the camp,
and her long, slender fingers would become tough
and calloused. She would *show* Luke van Meer that

there was less and less to jeer at once she had become adjusted to camp life. She still felt full of
energy, invigorated, if anything, by their verbal
skirmish. When Luke made her flare the adrenalin
started coursing round. Luke had the power to
stimulate her into anger or fear or ... or anything
else he chose. 'Anything else' was too dangerous a
reaction to define. Nor did she want to; her mind
shied away from erratic sensations she had never
experienced before and wasn't prepared to acknow-
ledge. Especially not after this morning's resolution.

Out of the corner of her eye she saw zipped boots
and denims. He had come to join her, watching and
more than likely waiting to continue taunting her
sardonically. But, glancing up warily, she found
that his manner was serious again.

'Selina, a word of advice. Stick to this part of the
river where it's flowing strongly. Don't go exploring downstream alone. There may be *magars* down
there where it widens and gets sluggish.' She rose
and looked enquiringly at him, and he translated
laconically: 'Crocodiles.'

She shuddered, 'I won't,' stepping back hastily
from the waterside. 'The python has taught me a
lesson!' Had it been only yesterday? Selina marvelled to herself. In this totally new environment she
had begun to lose track of time. Yesterday she had
been another girl on another planet, she thought
whimsically.

The grey eyes sparked with a humorous twinkle.
'No arguments? Well, thank God for that!' He
stooped and picked up the mugs. '*Magars* are fairly
safe, *liefje*, but not worth taking a risk. We'll take

a stroll down there and have a look when we've set up camp.'

'I'd like to help,' she offered eagerly, rubbing her wet hands briskly against her jeans, all animosity forgotten. This was the second time he had called her *liefje*. It didn't sound like a Hindustani word, and there was something about the tone, vaguely like a careless endearment, which put her off asking what it meant. She followed him back to the camp site.

As it turned out, she was more of a hindrance than a help, but she was keen to prove herself and to please Luke, and he and Narayan were remarkably patient with her bumbling endeavours. They had the essentials of camping pared down to a minimum of time and effort, and it was soon apparent that handling the heavier stuff and fixing the tents was entirely a job for the two men. Even the simpler task of untying rope knots defeated Selina, and she had to be content to lug cases and duffle bags around, find suitable places for the lanterns and utensils, and keep Patch from pushing his inquisitive nose into the food supplies.

She made an unsuccessful attempt to put up the folding camp-cot she had been using each night, and when she had fallen on to her tender knees on the stony ground twice, gritting her teeth against crying out, Luke came and hauled her to her feet.

He scanned her face, glowing from exertions. 'Okay, Selly, I reckon you've done your bit!' But the derision was very gentle and she laughed and scowled fearsomely at the camp-cot and said: 'I'll get this darned thing right if it kills me!'

She succeeded eventually. She would know how

to manage next time without making such a pro-
duction of it, she assured herself, flopping down on
the side of the cot and leaning back on her elbows
with a ridiculous sense of achievement; but as she
looked around the orderly camp, with Narayan sitting quietly in the sun reading a book and Luke
busy with some fishing tackle by the car, she had to
admit that her contribution hadn't amounted to
much. She giggled ruefully as Patch scrambled up
beside her.

Luke strolled over to her, carrying his fishing rod.
'Are you fit for a walk, or have you had enough for
one day?'

'I didn't do much, did I,' she sighed disgustedly,
getting to her feet. They set off downstream along
the stretch of loose stones and shale. She knew him
well enough already not to expect any polite pro-
testations about how hard she had worked, and there
were none forthcoming.

'It isn't your scene, let's face it,' he said bluntly.

'It could be.' She was filled with an ardent longing. 'Oh, Luke, it could be! It's just that I've never
tried—never had a chance to try anything like this.
It's like waking up after a nightmare and having to
learn to be *alive*. Give me a little time and you'll
see.'

He threw her a swift assessing glance. 'Physical
effort to release mental stress?' Picking up a stone,
he hurled it for Patch to chase.

'Yes—in a completely new atmosphere! It's so
different from everything I know, and fantastically
beautiful.' She took a quick breath. 'I wish it could
last for ever!'

'Nothing lasts for ever,' was his cynically brusque

response. Selina stood still, the bright ardour in her face wiped off by his rebuff. He stopped too, making a business of taking out and lighting a cigarette. After a few seconds he muttered wryly: 'Trust a fool to tell the truth at the wrong moment.' He thrust his lighter into his pocket and attempted an easier tone. 'I hope you'll feel the same way after a week of slogging up into the hills.'

'That won't last either, will it?' She bent to pick up another stone for the dog. The future was so doubtful, she couldn't begin to envisage it. She would take it as it came. The next hour, the next day. She pitched her stone for Patch. She had one certainty to cling to—she would never return to the clutches of Henry and Delia, whatever the circumstances. Luke had promised her that. But later on .... back in England on her own....

His hand closed around the soft flesh of her arm and turned her towards him. She was trembling slightly and his hand began to move gently up and down in a soothing motion. 'It's not going to be easy, Selly, shaking off the past and getting adjusted. But if you want to talk that nightmare out of your system——'

'No!' Her upward glance got caught in the intentness of his. She said slowly: 'Not yet, but thanks for the offer. Raking it all up just now would somehow spoil,' she gestured obscurely, 'all this.'

There was another pause in which he searched the vulnerable depths of her big violet eyes and she stood absolutely still, close to his large, virile frame, with the rough warmth of his hand on her arm, and felt renewed optimism flowing back to her. She smiled into his eyes and saw his expression change.

His grip tightened, then abruptly he released her.

He said: 'Well, at least you've made a start, cutting adrift.'

'You mean, burning my boats,' she responded brightly.

'Sure.' He feigned a light jab with his knuckles across her chin and chuckled. 'And as you've burnt your boats you may as well enjoy the fire!'

Further down, the river gradually widened into a quiet reach that must have been almost half a mile across, its banks spreading into open ground with clumps of bushes thickly covered with small white, sweet-scented blossoms and, here and there, graceful amaltas trees spilling over with long gold tassels, reminding Selina of laburnums in full bloom.

Luke touched her elbow and pointed towards a sandbank sloping away to the grey flow of water, and she could just make out a couple of long, dark, inert shapes basking in the slanting rays of the sun which showed up the rows of bony plates along their backs. A shiver ran down her spine and Luke's hand went down her forearm to link her fingers encouragingly.

'You can tell they're *magars* by the short, broad snout,' he told her in a hushed voice. 'They usually choose a quiet stretch like this; they don't like it where the current is too swift. Remember that and you'll be all right.'

'It would be terrible if a person got swept down there....'

'It would be risky. But they normally prey on smaller animals, even birds if they get the chance to snap them up.'

'I always imagined crocodiles with huge snouts

and long, vicious teeth!' she whispered, repelled yet fascinated by the reptilian shapes.

'That's another species called the *gharial*. It has a long, narrow snout and numerous curved teeth and lives in the larger rivers, like the Ganges, on the plains.'

At that moment, Patch came frisking out of the bushes, spotted the two crocodiles and started towards the water, barking dementedly. Selina screamed: 'Patch!' but it took a stentorian shout from Luke to bring the dog up short, muzzle extended, his legs quivering with tension. The crocodiles slid away, bodies writhing on leg stumps, into the grey water. Selina darted forward and caught hold of Patch, watching, mesmerised, as the rings of ripples heaved and broke up in the current; then she turned hurriedly as Luke called: 'Come on, let's go back.'

Not far from the camp site, where the river narrowed into eddies and deep rock pools again, Luke chose a boulder from which to fish.

'May I stay?' she asked hesitantly.

'Have you the patience?'

'Of course!' but it came out mildly. She was too happy to be provoked.

For a fleeting moment they looked into each other's eyes, and she could read his benign mood too. His eyes had the silvery grey light of the river; a flicker of humour without mockery which drew a soft sigh of contentment from her as she settled down in the lee of the boulder near him. The time slipped by, bridged by an occasional murmur of conversation between them. She felt enfolded in the purling sound of water, the call of birds, the faint, distant cry of some stealthy creature high up in one of the ravines. She pulled off her improvised scarf and let the breeze whip through her hair with the scented sweetness of flowers.

By the time the sun had westered behind the slope of the hill opposite, Luke had three plump fish. The temperature had dropped considerably, feathering little chills across Selina's back, and she was ready to return to the warmth of the camp fire and the snug comfort of blankets after some of the most serene hours of undemanding companionship she could remember.

If only this mood of Luke's would last! However arduous the coming weeks might prove, a few more golden afternoons like today's would give her the incentive to keep going.

Just how arduous it would be she was soon to learn.

CHAPTER SIX

MORNING brought such a clamour of unexpected
sounds that Selina sat bolt upright on her camp-cot.
Voices—a number of men's voices, calling out greet-
ings. Narayan's and Luke's talking in Hindustani.
Busy voices punctuated by Patch barking and the
clatter of hooves on rocky shale.

She was up in a second, lifting the tent flap to
peer out, round-eyed.

It was barely sunrise, but the site beyond the tents
seemed crowded with activity. There were six new
arrivals, two of whom looked like tough local hill
men and the other four of a rather different type
in khaki drill shirts and pants. With them were two
laden mules and a sturdy, toffee-brown pony. Patch
was jumping and yapping at one of the Indians as
if he knew him well. The others had set about un-
loading the packs, and as Selina watched, the mules
and pony were lightly hobbled and turned loose to
drink at the river.

Selina waited, curbing her curiosity for a few
more minutes while Luke and Narayan completed
their deliberations. The men drifted off to build a
fire of their own a little distance away, and squatted
down on the ground around the cone of sticks and
twigs which sent up a bright orange blaze of smoky
flames into the misty morning air.

Uncertain about venturing out, she called:
'Luke?'

He glanced her way. 'Stay put, Selly. I'll be with you in a moment.'

She was conscious of the men by the fire turning to look, then discreetly looking away. One of them got to his feet and came towards the tent; a wiry almost soldierly figure with grizzled hair, his crooked, stained teeth showing in a polite smile as he put his palms together in the Indian style of greeting.

"*Salaam, memsahib*. I am Kunwar Singh, the *sahib*'s servant. You would like I am preparing breakfast now?'

Nonplussed, she wavered: 'No ... yes ... I suppose so.' But it was enough to get him bustling with the coffee pot and stores box, with Patch frisking round him and getting in his way, a hindrance he seemed to put up with patiently as though he was used to the dog.

Luke strode over, pushing past her and dropping the tent flap behind him. His vast, stooping presence filled the canvas walls as he had filled the little car. He said: 'Sit down, Selina, or there won't be room to breathe,' but he wasn't amused about it. He sounded preoccupied.

She sat on the edge of the camp-cot, and as he lowered his weight cautiously beside her a feeling of trepidation ran like needles along her nerves. The cot creaked ominously as she inched away from him.

'Now listen to me, Selina.' His tone was terse and matter-of-fact. His easygoing mood had evaporated overnight and she tensed as he continued: 'There's no time for pussyfooting around any more. From here on, as far as anybody else is concerned—and that includes our own men and folks we run into on the climb in the next few weeks—you're my wife, Mrs van Meer, my *memsahib*. Savvy?'

She had been expecting this for the last couple of days, after what she had overheard, but hearing it from him as a sudden, brutally direct order stiffened her back with fury and dread. If he had broached it casually in a quiet moment, reassuring her as he explained the implications. . . .

'If by savvy you mean comprehend,' she said frigidly, 'no, I don't.'

'God Almighty! Is your head soundproof when it comes to listening to something you don't want to know?' he countered irascibly. 'In basic terms, we share the tent and anything else necessary. You stick by me, and you do as you're bloody well told.'

She flashed him a blighting glance. 'There's no need to be offensive!' Her heart was palpitating sickeningly, but she succeeded in adding in an insolently dismissive manner: 'The idea of sharing a small tent, like this one, with you is farcical. I wouldn't share a big one either. And when you say "anything else necessary", what precisely do you consider *necessary*?' The last word came out with freezing hauteur.

Grey eyes, flint-hard between narrowed lashes, held hers until his brows rose derisively and she dropped her glance.

He said: 'Is this the arrogant posturing you used on Henry Spender? You little simpleton! Don't you know that with a face and figure like yours it would be the sort of challenge a determined man couldn't resist?—to bring you down off your high horse and make you submit,' he laughed shortly. 'No conquest would be sweeter for a parvenu like Spender! Well, don't try those tactics on me, girl, because I'm a red-blooded barbarian myself, and you'll sure as hell get more than you bargain for.'

'Stop shouting at me!' she blustered belligerently while her mind grappled with the notion that her rebuffs had spurred Henry on instead of putting him off. It was probably true, she conceded silently with a little shiver, but how else could she have coped? She was too inexperienced to know what to do; and no one would *believe* her, let alone advise her.

Luke must have seen the shudder across her stiff shoulders. He thrust his hand into her tousled hair and turned her forcibly, disregarding her attempts at resistance. She jerked her head once or twice, but the pull on her scalp hurt and she gave up trying, sitting with her eyes shut and her mouth compressed. He stared down at the patchy pallor of her skin against which the bruising around her eye showed up in painful weals.

'Okay, okay!' he exploded a sigh of exasperation. Then his grip eased and his fingers curved more gently round the soft nape of her neck. The change from roughness to gentleness flustered her, yet she couldn't resist resting the weight of her head against his palm.

'I guess I sprang that on you hard,' his thumb and forefinger moved on the tendons of her nape, easing the tautness out of them, 'but I was hoping we could avoid this predicament. Now——' he shrugged.

'Something's happened?' Her eyes opened wide. She sat up straight. 'Those men out there?'

'Are our men, organised by our contact.' His hand dropped away from her shoulder. 'They were stopped on the way here by a couple of guys who claimed to be cops, asking questions.'

Selina swallowed convulsively. 'Questions?'

'About seeing an *angrezi* woman wandering around these parts. My servant and Narayan's had been briefed before leaving and swore that the only white woman they knew of was the wife of their boss on a trek up here. And they'd be flayed alive if they didn't deliver the fresh supplies on time. More questions. About the trek. Who and where to. They reckon they got away with it because they weren't held up for long, but I don't like the sound of it.'

'Do you think,' nervously chewing her lip, 'they'll follow them and check up on us?'

'Could be. Depends on what they're really up to: looking for Selina Roxley, or trying to keep tabs on Narayan and me. Either way, we'll have to make our story look good. The job we're on is vitally important, Selly. We've got to protect our cover at all costs.' His voice hardened. 'That means you co-operate, right? For your own protection, if you're not altruistic enough to feel you owe it to us,' he concluded with a caustic edge.

'You're despicable!' she accused him tremulously. 'First you try and scare me into doing what you wish, then you remind me that I'm beholden to you. It's b-blackmail!'

He said brusquely: 'Take it any way you want, but face up to it. You can't spend the rest of your life running out on situations you don't like, and I can't allow you to opt out of this one, it's too critical.' He watched her hunch forward, head bowed and hands pressed between her knees. 'So, whether you fancy it or not, Selina, you're my wife until the job's over. And we've got to make it convincing.'

'How—how convincing?'

He was silent for so long that she twisted her head up to look at him with all the bravado she could summon, but she was unprepared for the blazing rage in Luke's eyes. He said in a soft, threatening drawl: 'You reckon I'm on Spender's game?' and her boldness shrivelled in his searing anger.

'How do I know!' she exclaimed distraughtly. 'I had to be on the alert all the time. There was always some trick ... some pretext. ...'

She saw the gaze which had been raking her face with fiery needles transmuted into a cold, unwavering stare riveting hers until she began to feel breathlessly uncomfortable, and then confused, as if she had imputed something totally corrupt to Luke and should be cringing with shame.

She lowered her glance and said helplessly: 'Luke, I didn't mean to——'

'You meant to! I know exactly what you're driving at. If you're afraid I'll insist on sharing your bed as well as the tent, and force myself on you,' he rasped out abrasively, 'you'll have to take a chance and find out.'

He stood up, shoulders bent against the slope of the small tent, and she felt she couldn't bear the thought of this harsh acrimony between them. She blurted out desperately: 'All right, Luke, all right. I'll trust you!' What living in such close quarters with him would do to her own equanimity was beyond consideration at that moment. She had a strong urge to placate him. 'I'm sorry I misunderstood you,' she apologised in a low, pleading voice, 'but it's hard for me not to mistrust people's motives.'

After an awkward pause he said: 'I should have

realised that.' His tone and demeanour had altered
abruptly again. He raised her face, smoothing his
thumb over the crease between her delicate brows
with a light, impersonal touch. 'I told you once
before, you're safe with us. I won't harm you, Selly.
You can believe that without reservations.'

'Yes.' Relief washed over her, buoying up her
flagging spirit. 'And I'll do my best to help.' She
longed to press his hand to her cheek.

'Good.' He lifted the tent flap and spoke incom-
prehensively to Kunwar Singh, then returned to sit
beside her. 'We've got something for you.'

In a very short while the servant brought in a
box. He set it down at their feet and withdrew. Luke
met Selina's enquiring glance with a broad grin.

'Clothes, scraped together haphazardly in twenty-
four hours. God knows how they'll fit or what they'll
look like, but you need something warm and practical to see you through.' He opened the lid.

This was his 'remedy'! thought Selina, sliding
down on to her knees to finger the folded garments
with lively curiosity. 'How on earth did you manage
it?'

'Smoke signals, how else?' He sat observing the
fleeting expressions on her face as she scooped out a
pair of jodhpurs, some shirts, a couple of large pullovers and an Afghan jacket of the usual kind: thick,
shaggy sheep's wool inside and the coarse outer skin
decorated in patterns sewn in bright cotton thread.

Selina gave a little laugh and shrugged into the
jacket. It fitted reasonably well and was soft and
snug. 'It's a bit smelly!' Her nose twitched against
the animal skin as she tugged the neckline.

'Wait till it gets wet with a drop of rain,' Luke

warned, amused. 'They don't cure the skins any too well.' He peeled it off her shoulders. 'It'll keep your natural central-heating going in the cold, so don't be too finicky, Miss Roxley.'

'I'm too thankful to be finicky,' she said sincerely, looking into the humorous twinkle in his eyes. Suddenly she knew that the relief she had felt hadn't come from reassurance about his intentions towards her in this charade they had to play, but from reconciliation. He had been so very angry with her, not just annoyed or irritable or sarcastic, but in a rage which had made her shrink with distress. She needed the verbal cut and thrust to enliven her without wounding. And the spontaneous comradeship which had been growing between them was now becoming the breath of life to her; if it had all been destroyed so soon in the withering flame of Luke's anger she would have been lost.

Averting her gaze and holding up the jodhpurs, she began an enthusiastic inspection of the rest of the clothes. Luke told her the fawn-coloured breeches belonged to the schoolboy son of one of his friends, but the other garments were his own. The breeches looked a surprisingly good size for her, but when Selina dragged a V-necked pullover over her head the baggy result threw her into such a fit of the giggles that tears started in her eyes.

'It's good to hear you laugh,' Luke chuckled. He shook his head. 'I keep forgetting how young you are, but don't get hysterical, *liefje*!'

She sobered, brushing the moisture from her cheekbones. 'Please don't think because I was laughing that I'm ungrateful,' she said earnestly. 'I have a needle-and-thread case among my things and I'll put in some tucks and seams so that they don't look too obviously borrowed makeshifts.'

'A resourceful needlewoman?' came the familiar mockery.

'Quite good really,' she replied meekly, refusing provocation.

'Right.' He was brisk once more, tossing the clothes back into the box. 'I'll take you over to your private corner among the rocks, the men won't disturb you there. Put on the riding breeches, you'll be up on the pony when we hit the trail.' Then a quick afterthought: 'You do ride?'

'Not for a long time, but I've had lessons.' He moved to the tent flap, nodding as if satisfied, and she asked hastily: 'Can I rinse out some of my own bits and pieces, will there be time for them to dry?'

'Sure. When you're ready we'll have a good break-fast, and then do the sorting out and loading. I want to leave as soon as we can make it, but it will be an hour or two yet.'

Selina hurried her washing and dressing, think-ing wryly that she was not very fastidious these days. Well, a trek in the wilds was hardly conducive to being particular, and as long as she kept her body clean she could forget any fancy notions of good grooming. She pulled on the breeches, finding them a trifle loose but comfortable, added her own ranch shirt and Luke's old cardigan, belting it at the waist to make it blouse out and folding the sleeves neatly to make chunky cuffs on her forearms. She tied her mane of silky chestnut hair back on her neck with a silk handkerchief, slid on her sun-glasses to disguise her bruised eye and joined Luke and Narayan at the camp fire with mixed feelings of happy expectation and a vague apprehension about the so-called policemen making enquiries.

It was the most substantial breakfast they had yet had, prepared and served by Kunwar with smiling efficiency. He had somehow contrived tasty herb omelettes, had brought a loaf with him to make toast, and had bought milk from a herdsman along the way which made the strong coffee much more palatable to Selina.

Afterwards, she went into the tent to pack up and carried her case and the clothes box outside, but, with so many men around, there was nothing else for her to do. For a while she walked about restlessly with Patch at her heels, watching Luke and Narayan superintend the arrangement of the loads the mules had brought in, then drifted over to make friends with the toffee brown hill-tat she was going to have to ride. The pony tossed his head and blew suspiciously at her through distended nostrils, but eventually permitted Selina to stroke and pat him, and when she had fed him some small lumps of sweet *gûr* from the palm of her hand he seemed to accept her, nudging her greedily for more until she laughed and pushed him off.

Satisfied that she would be able to manage him, and feeling that she ought to be busy too, she collected her sewing things, a blue shirt and one of the pullovers Luke had donated to her wardrobe, and sat in the sunshine on a flat rock, near where she had spread out her own washing to dry. For an hour she soaked up the sun while she worked to give the garments a more wearable shape and fit. Her tiny pair of scissors were barely adequate and her fingers were pricked and rather sore, but the results were not bad, she thought smugly, not bad at all.

The camp had been dismantled and the gear now lay around in a sort of orderly chaos, being divided and reallocated into separate heaps. Selina could see Luke's towering figure moving cans of petrol, which must have arrived in one of the mule packs, over to the two parked vehicles, and she wondered what Luke was planning to do with the little car and the jeep. Feeling slightly disgruntled at being left out of the preparations, she came down from the rock and packed her handiwork and flimsy underwear, now dry, into her case. She wanted to ask Luke what was going on, but he seemed too occupied to be interrupted just to satisfy her curiosity. At the moment she might as well not exist for all he cared! she mused crossly.

She sauntered away from the noisy discussions and activity of the camp site, snapping her fingers in a game with Patch, then stopped and stared at the sight of an elephant lumbering through the trees by the cattle trail. As it came down to the river bank she noticed a man and a small child perched high on its shoulders behind the large grey head. Patch started to bark and the ears lifted like fans, the trunk swinging from side to side, then coming up restively against its head in what could have been an intimidating gesture. The *mahout* scolded and prodded it between the ears.

Patch would have darted forward, but Selina swooped on him, catching him in time, falling down and tipping sideways against a boulder.

'Selina!' Luke roared, scrunching the loose shale in his haste to reach her. 'What the hell are you doing? Are you hurt?' He bent over her.

For all his harshness, her heart leapt; he had been keeping an eye on her after all! 'No, just a bump,' she said lightly, and he straightened.

'Yes, well. . . .' Hands on hips, he watched the elephant moving slowly away along the riverside to a wider, quiet stretch. 'Don't go near them,' he slanted a stern glance down at her, 'and keep that damned dog under control.'

'What do you think I'm trying to do!' she protested, tightening her arm around Patch. But she couldn't work up any indignation about his peremptory tone because, in spite of all his other preoccupations, he had been genuinely, heartwarmingly concerned.

Luke stayed at her side for a few minutes. Selina was about to speak, but all his concentration was on the elephant, now wading into shallow water. Words which sounded like *'Dutt . . . Dutt!'* floated across to them above the sound of the river. At this staccato command the great beast halted. Other indistinguishable words brought the elephant down to its knees. The Indian dismounted and put his child and a bundle of possessions higher up the bank in a safe place under a shady tree, then turned to stand and survey the camp. Luke walked a short way the better to watch him.

Patch had subsided in the crook of Selina's arm, his muzzle resting on his forepaws, but his ears were twitching eloquently and every now and again his body quivered at the enforced restraint. The little brown child squatting under the tree couldn't have been more than two or three years old, wearing only a rag of shirt; the man, presumably his father, was

stunted, bow-legged, yet his dark limbs protruding
from a loincloth and stringy singlet must have been
strong to be able to control his huge mount, and
Selina was as captivated by this unusual trio as the
man himself appeared to be by the bustle of the
camp. Luke's interest seemed less cordial.

As she heard Luke call out to Narayan, the
mahout turned away, spoke to the child and took
what looked like a scrubbing brush from his bundle.
Then he encouraged the elephant to roll on to its
side in the shallows and proceeded to scoop up water
and scrub its thick, wrinkled hide. Selina pushed
up her sun-glasses and settled more comfortably
against the boulder, fascinated, until she became
aware that Narayan had joined Luke, and although
she couldn't hear their quiet dialogue she felt a
stirring of uneasiness. Was it possible that this man
had been sent to spy on them? Hardly credible!
And yet ... a frisson ran down her back ... it might
be a simple if outlandish method of obtaining information....

She was no longer watching the elephant-man
but Luke and Narayan, and a moment or two later
saw Narayan go down to the river for a chat. The
mahout continued splashing and scrubbing, grinning up at Narayan, gesticulating now and then as
they talked. He waded round to the bank, his manner became visibly more respectful. The chat went
on and looked quite amicable and Selina relaxed
a little. When Narayan started to walk back the
mahout directed another staccato flow of commands
at his elephant; the great grey bulk heaved itself
up obediently and rolled over to be scrubbed on

the other side, and Selina heard the child begin wailing plaintively.

'I think he is an honest peasant,' Narayan explained as he strolled towards Luke. 'Inquisitive, as they all are, for there is little to interest and cheer them in their hard lives. But no more than that. His wife has died and he has been to his village to fetch his son before returning to work on the plains. I have informed him that you two are wealthy Americans!'

Compassion welled up in Selina for the misery of the small, ragged infant, bereft of his mother, crying as he squatted patiently under the tree. All her instincts were to go and mop up his tears and comfort him for a while, if the dog could be safely tied up out of the way. 'Luke,' she began impulsively, 'could I——'

'No,' he said tersely, and she objected fiercely: 'You don't even know what I was going to say!'

'The answer is still, no. I can read your face like a book, *liefje*. Fussing over the child will embarrass them.' He looked at Narayan. 'But I guess we could spare some rice from our stores for them?'

'Much more practical kind of help,' Narayan agreed, and the two men went back to the camp site, leaving Selina sitting on the stony ground by the boulder feeling thoroughly snubbed.

However, her vexation didn't last long, for she was soon engrossed in another extraordinary sight. Having completed his task the *mahout* left his charge lying stretched out like a stranded whale at the water's edge, went up the bank to pick up his son and carried him to the elephant. He stood talking to the creature, in an almost confidential way, and then, to Selina's astonishment, put the tiny mite down firmly between the elephant's trunk and extended forelegs.

And there he stayed while his father kindled a fire under the tree and began to prepare some food. He had stopped crying and seemed to be playing quite happily with twigs and pebbles, and whenever his little half naked figure ventured away the elephant's trunk moved round him and drew him back with unbelievable gentleness. Selina was entranced. Where else in the world, she thought, could one see an animal as vast and powerful as a tank acting as nursemaid to a human infant? She had no doubt that if anyone had attempted to remove the child, that the gentle giant would have become a relentless adversary. The whole scene impressed itself on Selina's mind as another wonderful memory to treasure in the nebulous future.

'Selina?' Luke spoke softly beside her, breaking into her reverie. She looked up at him, her eyes still round and shining with pleasure, and said: 'Would you believe—an elephant as a baby-sitter?' and laughed with delight.

Luke scanned her face with an indefinable expression which had gone before she could take it in; he stooped and removed Patch from her grasp, tucking the dog under one arm as he held out his hand to pull her to her feet. She was still puzzling over his intent look when he said in the indulgent tone he used to comment or explain things to her: 'A *mahout* and his elephant are twin souls, dependent on each other and inseparable. Once they've been matched up they live and work together all their lives.'

She dusted her breeches. 'I can't visualise an elephant as a member of the household!' her voice lilted joyously at the idea. 'Family pets, dogs and cats, yes—but an *elephant*?'

He threw back his head, laughing. 'Sure, why not?' His arm came about her shoulders as they turned towards the camp. 'Elephants are social creatures. Very family-minded, even in the wild, very patient and caring with their young, not only their own particular babies but any calf in the herd. Every cow elephant functions as a protective "aunty" to all the youngsters if the need arises. I reckon the *mahout*'s son rates as "family" now.'

The clasp of his arm was not possessive, yet she was very conscious of it and there was a brief silence before she remarked stiltedly: 'It was wonderful to watch. I'm glad the elephant-man wasn't sent to spy on us.'

He quirked an enquiring brow at her change of tone, then said: 'No, Narayan's satisfied about that.' Kunwar Singh passed them on his way down to the *mahout*, carrying a paper bag. 'That'll be the rice we're giving him, and if he's questioned he'll tell them about the generous Americans he saw camping by the river!'

As they came into the camp site Luke's arm tightened for a minute or two, rather than releasing her, and Selina realised that it was intended as husband-and-wife behaviour for the benefit of their audience. Everything from the site and the roof rack of the car had been loaded ready for departure, the camping equipment on one mule, stores and cases on the other, and the men were waiting for orders. Narayan approached with the keys to the car and jeep. The

weight of Luke's arm was removed from Selina's
back as he set the dog down and, perversely, she
felt forsaken as he and Narayan and two of the men
went over to the empty vehicles.

The jeep left first, disappearing swiftly through
the trees with one of the new men at the wheel.
Selina wondered vaguely what would become of
it, then shrugged the thought aside; Luke and Narayan would dispose of it discreetly somehow, in their
own interests as much as hers. The little car made
a more dignified exit and Selina sighed to think
she would no longer be travelling in such close contact with Luke. Well ... why should that affect her?
she upbraided herself impatiently. He would be
around, larger than life. He would exhibit their
matrimonial status—as he had just now—whenever
he thought it necessary. And that would keep him
close enough.

Luke brought her an old, rather battered khaki
slouch hat with a hackle of faded feathers on one
side of the band, obviously his own, and much too
big for her head, but she contrived to wedge it on at
a jaunty angle by tucking up her thick hair at the
back. He put her up on the pony himself and as she
settled herself in the saddle and stirrups, he
shrugged into a light haversack and hung a camera
ostentatiously around his neck.

'Part of the camouflage!' he said sardonically,
adjusting the camera straps.

The party was moving off upstream with Narayan
and his servant who was acting as guide taking the
lead, followed by the hill men with the mules.
Kunwar Singh grasped a leading string on the pony.

'Are you comfortable?' Luke asked Selina, 'All set?'

'Yes,' she smiled at him from her perch, a renewed sense of excitement and anticipation sweeping over her. Luke whistled and clicked his fingers at Patch and they set off after the others.

They forded the river, showered with spray and deafened by the roar of the waterfall, and took a steep track through forests to the crest of the hill. Selina gave the valley a last, lingering glance. The trek had begun in earnest.

CHAPTER SEVEN

FOR interminable days Selina was almost too tired most of the time to be able to think straight, and practically fell into Luke's arms when he came to lift her off the pony for rest halts on the march and camp at sunset.

Muscles she had never used before ached dully and insistently as her delicate body adjusted to the hill-tat's gait. Climbing steep ascents she had to crouch forward over the pony's withers, clutching the pommel of the saddle, jolted with every clambering step up the trail. Her ears often popped and buzzed alarmingly with changes in air pressure and an unguarded glance at a precipice could make her head spin with vertigo. The sound of dislodged stones clattering away behind them like miniature landslides made her heart pound, although on one occasion a small rock-fall saved her. Disturbed by the passage of the mules, a venomous hamadryad reared up on the track, scales glittering black with pale chevrons, tongue flickering and hood dilated, poised to strike, when a shower of stones hurtled down and killed it—a chance in a thousand not even Luke could have anticipated.

Selina was considerably shaken and it took every ounce of spirit she could muster to keep going. Riding downhill again for long stretches put a different kind of strain on her body, feet braced and waist arched achingly to counteract the motion of the

pony. Tough, mountain-bred Toffee could take all
this literally in his stride, but after the episode of
the snake Luke emptied his haversack for Patch and
the little mongrel was carried on his back.

Up hill and down dale ... up hill and down dale
... the childish chant beat round Selina's mind as
she rode along doggedly for mile after weary mile.
Each day the guide and muleteers forged ahead to
set up camp. Luke would join Narayan for short
periods of the trek, but for the most part he and
Kunwar Singh escorted the pony, keeping up the
pace and making sure that Selina came to no harm.
Kunwar Singh seemed as tireless as the *paharis*, the
hill men, and would soon have a fire going and a
meal ready for the *sahibs* and *memsahib*, although
he shared the food and separate camp of the other
men.

It was exquisite relief when they sighted the
tents and Luke would swing her up into his arms
and carry her to the camp fire, propping her round
with blankets and sleeping bags for comfort. She
never uttered a word of complaint, mindful of
Luke's blunt comment that this kind of life was
not her scene and her own eagerness in assuring
him that it could be, if he would give her a little
time. But her long silences and dazed apathy had
told their own tale. There was no sparring, no
arguments; no laughter between them either. Luke
watched her perpetually, his expression grim and
tight-lipped at times, and when she could rouse
herself to think about it she was certain that he
regretted ever having set eyes on her, let alone
bringing her on this expedition.

And yet Luke was constantly encouraging her.

He was more patient than she could have believed possible, and because she felt so achingly stiff and weak she became completely dependent on him, even in the most intimate functions of washing, dressing and getting through each day. They might just as well have been husband and wife, except that there was no personal element. Luke nursed her along in a humane, practical, imperturbable manner which left no room for self-consciousness. Selina had never expected nor experienced such dispassionate attention from a man and accepted everything without demur, giving herself up gratefully into his care.

In the evenings she would relax entirely, see the sunset tide of rosy gold wash over the sky, feel the friendly presence of the dog pressed close to her side and stare at the changing pattern of flames in the fire with a kind of peace. If she stayed quite still her muscles would stop protesting and her mind become a tranquil blank. Luke and Narayan would talk quietly as Kunwar served the food, only sparing her occasional thoughtful glances to make sure she was eating enough. Then Kunwar would take the dog away and Narayan would tactfully move off to his own tent, and Luke would stretch her slowly and carefully on a blanket, and sit, until darkness fell, massaging her back and limbs very gently, easing the pain and stiffness out of them.

Those minutes in the brief blue-grey twilight of the Himalayas forged a strange bond, free of constraints. One evening Selina caught his hand in both hers, sighed deeply and confided: 'You're a *nice* man, Luke.'

'What an indictment! Niceness isn't a peculiarity

for which I'm known, and I didn't expect to hear
it from you.'

'Sneer if you like,' she shut her eyes drowsily, 'but
it's true.'

When he helped her prepare for bed, he usually
examined her scratches and bruises, which were
healing satisfactorily, and doctored the tender spots
galled by her saddle and stirrup leathers. Then she
slept exhaustedly from the time he tucked her in
on the camp-cot to the time he woke her in morning
light, with a mug of tea, to face another agonising
day.

There came a morning, at last, when she suddenly
awoke of her own accord and lay in the semi-
darkness listening to the first chinking bird notes
before dawn. Her body stirred with a faint revival
of the energy she had enjoyed prior to leaving the
valley for the hills. She tested her muscles. Bearable
... better than bearable! Her system was responding, the toughening up process was beginning to
work! Another day or two and she would be quite
accustomed to this strenuous routine, and prove to
Luke——

She stiffened at the sound of a rustling movement
near the camp-cot, a gusty intake and long, mur-
murous release of breath. Hitching herself up on
one elbow she peered nervously over the side and
saw the shadowy bulk in a sleeping-bag on the
ground.

Luke!——so he was sharing the small tent as he
had told her he would. She had been too knocked
out to register the fact before, but there was no
hostility left in her; on the contrary, his presence
was rather comforting. He was taking care of her,

keeping her safe, at night as well as by day.

A warm feeling, akin to affection, filled her as she
looked down at his sleeping face. The blunt, dur-
able, often sardonic features were indistinct, relaxed
in repose, with a pale gold stubble of beard blurring
the hard line of his jaw and a tangle of rough-cut
hair falling across his brow. This man—she leaned
nearer—this stranger she had met about two weeks
ago had been kinder and more forbearing and
seemed closer to her now than anyone else since her
early childhood.

Impulsively she stretched out a hand to brush the
hair from his forehead, then quickly withdrew it
without touching him. She rubbed her palm against
the edge of the cot in a fidgety, irresolute way. She
had no right to touch him, disturb him. And why
should she want to, anyway? Why should she suddenly feel the need to have him awake, lying beside
her and looking at her with that indefinable expression in his smokey grey eyes, talking to her,
perhaps reaching out to her. . . .

She moved very cautiously down to the end of the
cot and out of the blankets, wriggled into her
breeches and Luke's thick sweater and felt around
warily for her shoes. She endured a twinge or two of
discomfort as she straightened up outside the tent,
but the cold, pure air was gloriously invigorating
and she inhaled deeply and flexed her shoulders.
All at once it was good to be alive. A vaporous, an-
nular moon lingered above the dark, humped outline of the peak across the valley and the morning
star hung like a jagged sliver of ice against the
ashen sky. As Selina watched, daybreak began to
spread in milky light, the bird-song from the wooded

slope behind the camp became a steady crescendo,
and there was movement and a flicker of fire being
rekindled where the men were bivouacked a few
yards away.

Kunwar Singh padded over, hurriedly winding on
his turban. Patch fawned around her, and the
soldierly, old servant exclaimed: "*Memsahib*, you
are getting up too early! Please to sit—but not on
ground, the dew is heavy. I will be making the tea
for you. Not taking long.' He turned to scrape out
the embers of the camp fire and set up the kettle
on the Primus. His wayward English was unlike
Narayan's educated diction, except for a certain
intonation, but it was easily understood. He tended
to treat Selina in a fatherly way, and she liked him.

What Kunwar thought of his boss's eccentricity in
acquiring a woman out of nowhere, providing her
with some of his own clothing and carting her off on
a difficult Himalayan trek at the last moment, was
never apparent. His manner was always respectful,
and there was no doubt both Luke and Narayan
trusted his discretion. He probably knew the real
objective of the trek—which was more than she did,
thought Selina wryly. And that was another good
sign, she decided. Being aware of her surroundings
and looking for reasons; something she had been too
exhausted to think about recently. She was definitely
improving!

Declining to sit down, she thanked Kunwar with
a smile and strolled off into the woods for a few
minutes' privacy. At this height, the cold, misty
woodland was less forbidding, perhaps because the
trees were more open and familiar. Oaks, chestnuts
and deodar cedars; and patchy remnants of snow

in odd corners. Nevertheless, she didn't venture too
far in.

Luke was by the camp fire, an old jerkin over
his bare shoulders with the sleeves knotted about his
neck, wielding a battery shaver, and Narayan was up
too, filling water at the spring for his ritual ablu-
tions when Selina wandered out again. She felt
rather awkward at being around this early and in-
truding on them, and veered off towards the hobbled
pony and mules.

'Selly!' The bellow brought her up short. 'Come
back here.'

The tone of it put her back up. For the first time
in ages she was regaining a bit of vitality and independence, and what did Luke do? Shout at her as
if she were a coolie! He should have been glad to
see her making an independent effort, she thought,
as she sauntered over glowering haughtily at him.

'Are you annoyed because I'm not hanging around
your neck like an invalid this morning?' she queried
crossly.

'If irritibility is a sign of convalescence, you must
be on the mend,' he remarked, chuckling. He put
the shaver away, looked up. 'So that's where my
sweater's got to!'

'Oh-h. . . .' In her mind's eye she saw his sleeping
face in the dimness of the tent, and her own sudden
need to touch him or move right away returned so
strongly that she swung towards the tent, saying:
'Sorry. You were—you were still asleep and it was
the nearest I could reach. I'll go and change.'

'Leave it, have some tea.' He took one of the
mugs from Kunwar and handed it to her. Then he
stood appraising her thoroughly from top to toe,

taking in her mane of tousled hair, the peach flush
of her new tan; brighter eyes and tilted chin, and
a much steadier, straighter stance.

She shifted uneasily under his shrewd inspection
and burst out tartly: 'Do you think you'll recognise
me next time you see me?'

'Mm-m. By the look of you deterioration in
temper equals improvement all round.' The irony
sparked at her over the tea-mug he lifted in a mock
salute. 'Welcome back, Miss Roxley!' He drank his
tea at a gulp and handed the mug to Kunwar. 'And
keep away from the hill men and their mules.'

She bridled again. 'Why?'

His brows shot up. 'Why is it always—why?'

'Because you hand out your edicts like the word
of God. I'm entitled to a rational explanation,' she
said loftily, and took a sip from her mug.

'Okay,' he said. 'Fleas.'

'*Fleas?*'—almost choking on the hot tea.

'As simple as that. *Pulex irritans*, the human flea.
If you don't want to spend your time scratching
yourself, and searching your clothes, keep your distance.' Luke removed her half empty mug to a safe
place.

Selina was staring at him with such round-eyed
horror that he took her face between his hands and
began laughing. She stiffened, then laughed weakly
too and rested her cheek against his large, rough
palm.

'You're pulling my leg again. I never know
whether you're teasing or not.'

'Maybe I was teasing a little. When you put on
the Haughty Hannah act I can't resist it. But fleas
are easy to pick up, *liefje*.' She grimaced with dis-

gust and he added briskly: 'It's not an earth-
shattering problem, you little dummy! Just a bit of
extra care and cleanliness and we'll be okay.' He
gave her a gentle push towards the tent. 'Now go and
dress. Can you cope on your own today? Right. And
—hey!——' Selina poked her head from the tent
flap. 'Chuck my sweater out as soon as you can.'

Still shuddering occasionally, Selina shook out
and investigated each garment carefully before putting it on again, yet the thought must have stuck
at the back of her mind and made her nerves jumpy
because as they set out on the dusty track after breakfast her skin began to itch, first here, then there, for
no reason at all, and she had the greatest job in
the world to resist a frantic urge to scratch, conscious that Luke was walking behind the pony and
would notice and roar with laughter.

But her twitchy nerve-ends were instantly forgotten as they reached the brow of the hill. The sub-
lime immensity of the view made Selina gasp. The
air was so clear and rare that she could see endless
peaks and ranges soaring, fold upon fold and ridge
upon ridge, to the distant north. Dense green,
forested hills merged into chains of blue and brown
mountains, which in turn were surmounted by
snow-streaked domes poking through trails of low-
lying cloud. And to cap this breathtaking perspective were the high, icy crests and glaciers of the
Eternal Snows glittering against the sky.

It was the most magnificent and humbling sight,
and left Selina feeling as though they were human
ants crawling on the backbone of the world. When
she had got her breath back she half-turned in the
saddle, her eyes round and dark and glowing.

'Oh, Luke, it's incredible—and if it hadn't been for you I would never have seen it!'

He came alongside the pony. 'It's a fine view from here, but it's only an infinitesimal part of the greatest mountain system on our planet.'

'How high are we, here, Luke?'

'As the Himalayas go, we're at the bottom of the ladder, Selly. Not more than about seven thousand feet. That's why these areas in Gharwal and Kumaon are called the "hills". It's a long, long way to the giants like Everest.'

'And that range over there, across the valley?'

'I would reckon about nine thousand. We won't be going much higher than that.'

'Luke...' she hesitated a second, 'just where *are* we going?' she asked carefully.

He didn't reply at once but stood staring across the panoramic view. Couldn't he trust her now that they had come so far and shared so much? she thought bleakly. Obviously not, for he evaded the question by saying: 'There's a good way to go yet. You won't find it so hard now you're beginning to get your second wind.'

Her fingers tightened on the rein. 'I wasn't complaining,' she told him stiffly.

'No. I know what you're asking, but I can't answer that—yet.' He turned and laid a hand on her knee for a moment. She tweaked the rein and made the pony move away restively.

'If you can't trust me,' she flared up exasperatedly, 'why don't you say so! All along there's been this——'

'For God's sake quit picking a fight on a beautiful day like this,' he cut in sharply. Then he looked up at her and his eyes glinted with humour. 'Sure, we had doubts about you at one time, Selly,' he said on an easy, bantering note, 'thought maybe you'd been deliberately planted on us. Crashing the jeep was no put-up job, but we had you checked out all the same!'

If he had been hoping to goad her into indignation or laughter, he had failed. What was the matter with her? she wondered glumly. She was still not quite herself, perhaps. She wanted, more than anything at this moment, to feel she was sharing everything with Luke—his plans and problems as well as her joy in the majestic scenery and their daily existence together.

Something of this must have shown in her face. His expression changed, the humour disappearing as he asserted brusquely: 'What I said before still goes. You're not getting involved. We've done everything possible to cover ourselves, but there's no cast-iron guarantee that the assignment is going to work out, and the less you know about it the safer you'll be.' His tone lightened. 'You concentrate on protecting your identity. Enjoy each new experience. Make the most of it, shake off all the old hang-ups, huh?' He paused, then added gently, significantly: 'Selly, you're going to be okay, whatever happens. Understand? If I don't make it personally, you'll be well looked after, I promise you that, *liefje*.'

This attempt to reassure her inflicted a shock she was unprepared for. Selina dug her heels into the pony's flanks, urging him forward, to hide the sudden consternation in her face. She had been so taken up with her own miseries and concerns that although she had known the job Luke was on was

difficult, secret and risky, the notion that he might
actually be endangering his life hadn't entered her
head. Until this awful moment.

That was what he had implied, wasn't it? *Whatever happens ... if I don't make it personally....*

Luke was intent on shielding her, come what may;
but not himself. Was there a serious element of
danger in their mission? If so, he was walking
straight into it—he and Narayan. And he might
not survive. And there was no hope of arguing or
pleading with him, to find out what was really going
on or try and dissuade him from it.

Shaken by the emotional force of a new anxiety
she hadn't thought of or felt before, she rode away
from him without looking back, her mind in a
turmoil. She had been thinking of herself, been
afraid for herself, far too long—nobody else to
consider or worry about, nobody with any emotional
claim on her since her old nurse had been dismissed
and her father had died. Now she was facing the
painful discovery that Luke van Meer had become
the one being in the world who mattered to her,
not merely as the man who had rescued and given
her her freedom but as a friend in a unique relation-
ship which would never occur again. He had secured
a future for her. But without the certainty that Luke
would be there, somewhere, to turn to, that future
would be as bleak and barren as the hilltop they
were descending in stony hairpin bends.

The sun burned down through the thinner atmosphere. Eagles and vultures floated on the thermals
from the valley, then swooped out of sight below the
tree. At one point they were plunged into the heart
of a low cloud rising in wisps of vapour up the

hillside. After traversing a ridge they reached
slopes of grass and wild raspberry brambles, and
tumbling outcrops of ancient volcanic rock rearing
up in weird shapes. As it was well past midday
there were lengthening shadows among the rocks
providing shade and places to rest, and Luke and
Narayan called the usual halt.

Luke helped Selina off the pony. She slid down
to her feet against the big, solid length of him. His
supporting hands were warm and hard under her
arms and he smelt of dust and the heat of the sun.
He was as familiar and dear to her now as if she had
known him since her childhood. She swayed forward, leaned on his chest and closed her eyes, willing him to hold her close and dispel the wretchedness
that had racked her for hours, and when his arms
went round her she heaved a long, quivering sigh.

What was that name he called her? she mused
absently for a second or two. Deeply spoken, sounding like 'leef-yer'. She had heard it often enough,
but it had been different this morning; somehow
softer, more expressive. She would ask him what it
meant—not just a superficial translation but what
he had been *saying* to her by using it in that particular way.

She clutched his bush shirt and pressed her body
to his regardless of the camera, which he kept slung
round his neck, digging into her. Her head tilted,
she opened her mouth to whisper her question when
he startled her by gripping her arms, jerking her
away and dumping her roughly, decisively on her
heels. If it hadn't been for the pony she would have
fallen backwards.

'Change of tactics?' he derided in a harsh, sardonic tone he hadn't used for so long that Selina felt as if he had struck her in the face.

She gaped in bewilderment, inexpressibly hurt. 'What tactics? What are you talking about?' She would never comprehend, much less get used to Luke's abrupt shifts in mood.

He said tersely: 'Come on, don't give me that big-eyed naïvety! You've spent the morning sulking because you couldn't find out what you wanted to know. But if you think you'll wheedle the information out of me with a bit of female inducement you've got another think coming. You'll be told what this trek is all about when the time comes, and not before.'

'Is that what you think?' she gasped, anger flaring up like the colour that surged into her face at the way he had misunderstood and rejected her spontaneous gesture of troubled affection. 'Sometimes you're unpardonably—crude! I wasn't sulking, I was feeling hot and tired,' she claimed disdainfully, 'and you usually help me. I'll try to be more independent in future.'

Luke stood watching her, hands on hips, with a look in his narrowed eyes which made her turn away, clenching her fists at the mocking disbelief. She put Toffee's reins over his head and slapped the pony's rump to send him off the path to graze. She said in a cold, hard little voice: 'As long as I get out of this and back to England safely, I couldn't care less what you're up to!'

The lie stuck in her throat, suspending her voice as she stalked away to a rock nearby and flopped in the shade. She tipped the brim of Luke's old hat over her eyes, blinking at the sting of tears. Patch

barked and scampered over the grass to snuffle
around her, then lay back panting, his tongue
lolling out. She could have got up and fetched him
some water to drink, but felt too miserable and
played out, still consumed with worry about Luke
and upset by the unpleasant little scene.

Her own safety was no longer important to her.
His was. But how could she explain the realisation
which had hit her so cruelly? He had chosen to mis-
interpret a sincere if sentimental feminine expression of concern and regard for him as a disgustingly
scrubby kind of artifice—like making cheap ad-
vances. Luke of all people; the only person with
whom she had thought she could now be completely
natural and honest. The rebuff came as an unbear-
able blow both to her feelings and her pride. What
on earth had become of the pride which had carried
her through so many ugly predicaments in the last
few months? she wondered woefully, flicking an ant
off her arm.

Kunwar brought her some food and a cold drink,
and a pan of water for Patch. She nibbled an apple,
swallowed the freshly squeezed lime juice with water
thirstily. Luke and Narayan sat in the shadow of an
adjoining rock, eating as they talked over the map
spread out before them, and she squinted under the
broad brim of her hat at the strong, sun-tanned
features until Luke looked up directly at her. Pointedly averting her head, she fixed her gaze on a
colour-spangled butterfly fluttering, then gliding on
a breath of air, fluttering again and settling on a
cluster of bramble blossoms. Beautiful, short-lived
creature dancing in the sun; Selina rubbed her hand
over her eyes. On the heights the atmosphere made

every colour richer, every outline sharper; even in her unhappiness each little detail delighted her.

She managed to catch and mount the pony before Luke had time to shrug into his haversack and assist her. It was gratifying to have his mobile brows shoot up in surprise as she rode on to the track, but she was not so pleased to see the surprise replaced by a knowing gleam of amusement and hustled the sure-footed hill-tat downhill after the mules at a well-nigh reckless pace. It was childish, and she knew it, as she also knew that she would have to come to some sort of truce with Luke or life would become intolerable. But she would keep aloof for as long as she could.

Streams gushed over crags, and through scrub meadow, and small fishes with suckers clung to the rocks in the swirling currents. The track soon entered the tree-line, a forest of evergreen rhododendrons, some as much as forty or fifty feet high, which were already beginning to show fat buds opening into rose-purple flowers. Presently the path joined a proper road circling the valley from the east, and although it was unmade the surface was well-worn and the gradient considerably easier for riding. It was wider too. No need now for segregation in single file.

Selina was aware that Luke was catching up and intended walking beside the pony, but the party had to draw in towards the slope to allow a gang of *paharis* to pass with their heavy loads. These hill men were red-brown of skin, stocky and as wiry as monkeys in their ragged pants and jackets. Each man had a large, cone-shaped *kundi* basket on his back attached to a webbing strap which went around his forehead so that his head, neck and shoulders took the weight. One or two of the coolies were mere boys, and Selina marvelled at their strength in carrying loads in this strange fashion.

Narayan hailed Luke and after a hasty conversation which Selina couldn't hear, they had a friendly exchange with one of the older hill men. Most of them stopped, backs bowed under their loads, and Luke passed a pack of cigarettes round. They resumed their uphill trudge. Selina turned in the saddle to watch the slow procession climbing the road and saw the tough, knotted muscles in the men's calves bulging with strain. The last man shouted a farewell, grinning up at her.

She flicked the reins to get Toffee moving again and was near enough to hear Luke tell Narayan: 'If the Bhutia hadn't yet opened up his hovel and started trading when they came through the pass, Bala Sen's schedule seems about right. At this rate we should have a day or two in hand.'

He and Narayan then walked on ahead, still talking. More mysteries! thought Selina bitterly. For the first time Luke had abondoned her on the trek with only Kunwar Singh walking a discreet pace behind to keep her company. Well! in her embarrassment and resentment about this morning's clash between them she had asserted her independence, and Luke was taking her at her word.

She was still thinking about this when she left the camp site in a clearing above the village in the valley to find a secluded spot to wash off the grime of a hard day's ride. Previously Luke had selected the place she used each day, but he was standing by the other tent engaged in another lengthy discussion with Narayan—probably mulling over the information they had gleaned from the *pahari* carriers and planning their future strategy. So Selina collected her things from her case and went off boldly on her own.

The sound of running water drew her down into a sheltered ravine where a little rill bubbled through a rocky dell thickly green and moist with ferns and speckled with white butterfly orchids. It was a beautiful spot hidden among the trees. She was soon out of her clothes and enjoying the refreshingly cold, crystal clear water.

Towelling herself quickly, she got dressed and had just rinsed out her underwear when she felt a crawler on her bare forearm and saw what looked like a worm looping and stretching before it fastened on to her skin. She shook her arm to throw it off, then jerked agitatedly, then brushed at it frantically with the bundle of clothes, but it had stuck fast. She tried to poke it with a twig. It wouldn't budge. Hysteria began to rise and choke her as the bottom end of the loathsome blob became slightly distended.

Faint with fright and revulsion, she clambered up the bank and stumbled through the trees towards the camp site, clamping her teeth on waves of nausea. 'Luke....' her voice came out in a thin moan. He turned, and with a sharp expletive at the sight of her chalk-white face, hurried to reach her. Unable to say any more, Selina held up her arm.

'Okay,' he relaxed on a gusty breath. 'Okay, don't panic, it's a leech.'

He took the tin of salt from a box, trickled some on the bloodsucker. As Selina watched, her stomach heaving, the leech started to dissolve in a dribble of blood and fell off. Luke kicked the remains into the fire.

Selina stammered: 'I t-thought I was being p-poisoned. . . .'

'Not from those. No harm done, but we'll check for any others.'

He led her into the tent, examined her limbs and clothing and, once he was satisfied she hadn't picked up any more, cleaned the spot on her arm.

'Ugh-h-h! It was slimy . . . beastly. . . .' She was still shuddering with reaction. She burst into ignominious tears and he gathered her close and let her cry it out. 'Luke, I'm sorry,' she sniffed dolefully, 'for this morning . . . now all this,' and he held her away, scowling down in mock ferocity.

'If it ever happens again I'll give you something to cry about!' He hugged her tightly, then released her and brushed the tears from her cheeks.

Selina laughed shakily, happily. They were friends again.

CHAPTER EIGHT

Two evenings later they were camped by a river in a deep gorge. They had avoided contact with the village in the upland valley—except for a brief foray by Kunwar Singh who had returned with eggs, a stringy chicken and some goat's meat to supplement their provisions—and had taken the road down into a long river rift cutting through the mountains. From here they were following the track which ran alongside the river for many miles.

If not entirely happy, Selina was content to exist from one day to the next. She had ceased to think about her appearance. She used only cream or suntan oil on her skin and a little lipstick to prevent her lips from getting dry and cracked. She felt fit and energetic too; Luke had been very strict about what they drank and how their food was handled, and about taking prophylactic pills, so that they had escaped debilitating stomach complaints. Now that she had got rid of her unsightly bruises and that drained look of exhaustion, her skin had taken on the bloom of a peach, her large eyes were clear and lustrous and her hair had become an even thicker mane of burnished chestnut; and without pain and stiffness she had regained her flowing natural grace of movement and her unconscious air of haughty elegance.

She had long since forgotten her wrist-watch and lived by sunrise, noon and sunset like the rest. Time had lost its meaning here in the empty vastness of the Himalayas. For Luke as well, it seemed. He was very genial and even tempered these days. She must have imagined the oblique inference that Luke was somehow risking his life in this venture. Or maybe she had exaggerated the significance of what he had said that morning, she pondered reflectively, lounging by the fire and drying her hair with a rough towel after shampooing it in the river. He had probably been trying to break it to her gently that he might be too busy once this expedition was over to take her back to England personally. He would arrange everything but couldn't be sure of carrying it through himself.

If only she could ask him if that was what he had meant! She didn't dare broach it again. The last thing she wanted was to annoy him and spoil their companionship. She was more self-reliant, but Luke was invariably at her side and always within reach—as necessary to her now as the air she breathed. The very thought of separation was a dark cloud on her horizon. Terror that he might lose his life had abated; but the fear that she would inevitably be losing him to his own private life, about which she knew absolutely nothing, oppressed her. And the fact that his attentions were so circumspect, so calmly impersonal, had begun to make her feel vaguely restless and dissatisfied.

Selina tossed the towel aside, took her brush and ran it through her thick, silky hair, parting it into sections and fanning out the strands to the warm air from the fire. She was bending forward, her face hidden, when Patch scrambled up and jostled her arm as he rushed past her barking in a shrill, aggressive way. She shook her hair back, smoothing it with her hands as she looked over her shoulder. A party of about six people with a gang of laden porters were coming up the river track, silhouetted against the flush of the evening sky.

Luke and Narayan exchanged glances and immediately rose, putting away maps and notes they had been studying by the other tent. As they set off towards the newcomers, Luke roaring at the dog to come back and be quiet, Selina noticed that there were women in the group—European women, from what she could see at that distance. With a swift recoil at the unexpectedness of it, she jumped up and fled into her own tent.

For minutes she sat on the camp-cot uncertain what to do. What would Luke want her to do? Would he call her out? Would she have to face these strangers? Chewing her bottom lip nervously, she heard footfalls getting nearer, voices growing louder. And then Luke's, clear and surprisingly cordial, with a deliberately accentuated North American drawl, suggesting that the newcomers set up camp on a much wider clearing he had observed further up the track as he came downstream. She was leaning towards the tent flap to peep out when she heard him jovially accepting an invitation to visit their camp later, after they had settled in and had a meal. She drew back and sat as quiet as a mouse, hoping she had escaped notice and wouldn't have to accompany him and Narayan.

The hope was short-lived. There was more talk, a ripple of polite laughter. The voices faded and a few stones rattled down the track as feet tramped

away. Luke whistled up the dog and came to find
Selina.

'No use hiding,' he said as he ducked into the
tent. 'They spotted your retreat and the women are
as inquisitive as magpies. I told them you'd washed
your hair and were too shy to come out, but they
insist on meeting you and you'll have to put in an
appearance with us tonight.'

She looked up at him, dismayed: 'Oh, Luke, must
I?'

'Less chance of gossip and conjecture if you do.
Hey now, Selly, you can carry it off. Rustle up your
best gear and put on all your social graces and you'll
get away with perjury in a good cause!'

'If you say so,' she agreed dubiously, 'but it's going
to be dreadful trying to make conversation. How
much can we say ... who are we? ... I mean....'

'Get dressed and we'll discuss it over supper.'

Selina fished out the fashionable slacks and match-
ing sweater in peacock blue she had worn on the
plane travelling to Delhi, changed into them and
then searched her handbag for the cosmetics she
hadn't used for so long. Although her hand was a
bit tremulous she succeeded in applying a light
touch of make-up which made her look less like
a scruffy waif, she thought, peering into the mirror
of the compact with a nervous giggle. Tying her
one and only scarf over her unruly hair, gipsy-style,
she slipped on the Afghan jacket and joined the
two men by the fireside.

It was absurd to feel self-conscious at being so
mildly 'dressed up', but she did, and the twinkle of
amused appreciation in Luke's eyes was no help.
'Aren't you going to get into something more re-

spectable?' she challenged him imperiously, to mask her shyness.

'Atta girl! That's the way to slay 'em!' he commended with a maddening grin. 'Come and sit on this box where you won't muss up that well-bred exterior. Narayan and I will smarten ourselves up after supper to provide you with a suitable escort, Your Royal Highness.'

'Oh, Luke, don't tease.' Self-consciousness and disdain vanished. She sank on to the box. 'I'm scared stiff!'

'A little preparation now, and a little tact and mendacity later on. No big hassle, dummy! We won't hang about, just visit long enough to show willing and divert suspicion. And find out all we can at the same time, though they seem harmless enough. Okay?'

She sighed. 'Ye-es, all right,' and took the plate of rice and a light, delicious curry Kunwar was offering her.

Selina's confidence slowly built up during the meal. Kunwar had already lighted the hurricane lanterns and there were beams of illumination from the newcomers' camp up-river, but the dusky shadows along the gorge offered a kind of refuge. It would be easier meeting them—and lying to them! —in semi-darkness than in daylight.

Luke said: 'Now this is the scenario, Selly. I'm a pharmacologist on a particular line of research here in India, studying the action of certain drugs on the body. I went to London early this year for a conference—do you know London, Selly?'

'Not very well, but I've been there a few times. My father had a large estate in Hampshire and sometimes took me with him as a treat when he had to go there on business. And I've been to London to buy clothes.'

'That should do.' He handed Kunwar his plate. 'Okay, so we met in London. Let's say it was a party given by mutual friends. Love at first sight,' he said mockingly, 'we were married by special licence, and I brought you back with me. We didn't have time for a honeymoon. Back in Delhi, Narayan recommended a short leave trekking in the hills and offered to mastermind the arrangements so that you and I aren't burdened with mundane details. Very considerate about the Western notion of honeymoons, our friend Narayan!' he chuckled. 'Do you think that's sufficiently romantic to sidetrack the women from the real background?'

'I—I suppose so.' She turned to the Indian who was nodding with quiet amusement. 'And Mr Narayan, what does he do? If anyone should ask.'

'I am Dr van Meer's associate, deputed by my government to facilitate in every way his—er—researches. A liaison officer, you may say.'

'Also a close and generous friend,' Luke added. 'Got all that? Except for your part in this, Selly, there's enough truth to make our cover stick. Just play the loving young newlywed. Demure and not very forthcoming.' He quirked an ironic brow. 'I reckon if you bat those big round eyes at them and look shy and reserved, they'll lay off too many personal questions.'

That seemed as much as they could anticipate. The two men would handle any other awkward enquiries. They were getting up to go and change when Selina had a sudden thought. 'Luke, a ring—

I should be wearing one. If they're European women they'll expect to see a wedding ring....'

'Hell! I never thought of that. Have you got anything with you?'

'I was wearing a couple on the flight out, dress rings, but I took them off and put them away at the rest-house. I remember! I wrapped them up and hid them....' she paused. 'In my bag ... yes, in my handbag.' She ducked into the tent and brought it out, rummaging in the inner pockets and pulling out a tight little squirl of tissue paper. 'They're here safe, thank goodness! Oh, what about this eternity ring? I'd forgotten I had this one too.'

She showed them the gold circle inset with diamonds all the way round. It was very valuable and looked it, and Luke whistled through his teeth. 'That should make the poor folk sit up and take notice,' he drawled dryly. 'Here, give it to me.' He took it from her, picked up her left hand and slid it on to her finger, and Selina felt an odd shock deep inside her, so painfully sweet that she pulled her hand away, avoiding Luke's eyes.

'It seems all right,' she said unsteadily. 'Suitable, I mean.'

'Yeah, suitable.' The response was heavy with sarcasm. 'One look, and they'll figure the bridegroom must have robbed a bank.'

Confused by her feelings and stung by this mordant comment, Selina snapped back: 'Will it do, or not?' She forced herself to meet his eyes.

There was a glitter, hard and inimical, between his eyelids, reflected in points of light from one of the lanterns. She caught her breath, pressing her lips together because she wanted to cry out: 'Why

are you angry? *Why?*' It had sprung up so rapidly,
this tension between them, that her mind reeled
for a second and her heart started to race.

'Will it do?' she repeated at last, staring at him
defiantly.

Their glances held each other at bay a moment
longer, then clung with a passionate intensity that
drove all coherent thought out of her head. She
put out a questing hand, laid it against his chest
without knowing what she was about. Luke's compelling gaze moved slowly down to the soft, vulnerable curves of her mouth, and she shut her eyes,
taking a shallow breath and waiting ... waiting....

For what?—consternation swept over her as
Luke's harsh voice jarred her back to her senses.
'Who gave you this expensive bauble?' he demanded cynically, lifting her hand by the ring
finger and holding it away from his chest with in-
sulting emphasis.

'Oh-h-h ... the ring?' It was an effort to think
about that now. 'My father. Well—I mean, it's been
in the family a long time—I mean, it belonged to
my mother and when I was old enough Father gave
it to me.'

'Make up your mind,' he said curtly. Then, 'I
guess it'll do.' He dropped her hand with a shrug
and went into the tent to change his clothes.

Selina drooped on to the box-seat again. Her
heart had slowed down, leaving her with a bleak,
empty feeling. She thrust her hand into her pocket
and clenched her fingers until the gold band dug
into her flesh. Luke, who could be so kind, could
also be deliberately cold and brutal. What on earth
did it matter who gave her the ring? Did he think

Henry Spender had been lavishing extravagant gifts on her? Worse still, did he believe *she* would accept that sort of gift?—that she was one of those vulgar, odiously acquisitive harpies who conned men out of jewellery for favours they had no intention of giving?

It had been implicit in Luke's offensive manner; and coming, as it had, on top of an uncontrollable wave of emotion, made her cheeks burn with mortification. Twice Luke had repelled and affronted her like this. Twice in recent days, and she was too downcast to consider why or fight back.

The newcomers' camp was about a quarter of a mile up-river. There was no moonlight yet within the walls of the gorge and Kunwar Singh led the way with a lantern, Selina walking between Luke and Narayan along the rather narrow uneven track behind him, and Patch snuffling close at their heels. From the quiet dialogue of her companions Selina, silent and aloof, learned that the other group consisted of a British married couple, an Indian zoologist and his Danish wife and an Australian photographer. The zoologist and photographer were apparently working on a project for the World Wildlife Fund.

Quite an international gathering, Selina noted wryly, bracing herself not only to be sociable but to act out this bogus whirlwind romance Luke and Narayan had dreamed up. She was not in the mood for either after Luke's perplexingly boorish behaviour. As the lights and glowing camp fire drew nearer and figures could be seen moving on the little shelf of open ground under the cliff, her stomach contracted nervously. She had no idea what

Luke would expect of her. She would leave it to him to make the first move in this distasteful charade.

They had to climb a bank of scree up to the camp. People were coming hospitably towards them. Selina's foot slipped on the loose stones and the next instant Luke's arm was clamped round her, drawing her up and holding her tautly against him. He turned her into his shoulder and she could feel the heat of his body through the bush shirt under her cheek. He lowered his head to hers, brushing his jawline over her brow, cradling her more gently until the stiffness drained out of her and she gave in completely, all the hurt and constraint washed away in blissful relief.

'Selly?' He tilted her face. 'All right now?' he murmured, and she knew he was not referring to her clumsy mishap on the scree. She nodded mutely because of the lump in her throat, and touched the hand under her chin with tentative fingers. Luke stroked his rough palm over her cheek, then half led, half carried her into the camp. This bit of unintentional by-play had not been lost on the friendly group awaiting them, to judge by their smiles, and even if Luke had shrewdly used their reconciliation for an appropriate display of devotion, she was too happy and relieved to care.

Luke introduced her merely as 'my wife', and as she shook hands and tried to take in the names of the others she realised that it would have been imprudent to introduce her as Selina, or Selly. There was no knowing where these people were going or who they might contact, and the casual mention of her name elsewhere might ring a bell and give the game away. Nevertheless, the formal 'Dr Lucas van

Meer and Mrs van Meer' sounded strange.

The stout little Englishwoman organised them around the campfire. 'Not enough camp chairs. Don't as a rule run into other trekkers, you know, not so early in the year.' She was plain and practical, from her square-cut greying hair to her thick ribbed stockings and brogues. 'You sit here, Mrs van Meer. I'll manage with a cushion. Used to this sort of life, you know.'

Selina had started to protest when Luke cut short the polite argument by sitting down with his back against a stores box and pulling Selina into the crook of his arm down on the disputed cushion, settling her beside him. Taken aback, she sat rigidly for a moment or two while a gust of jocularity about newlyweds brought a hot flow of colour to her face. But the humour was kindly and the atmosphere free and easy, and she surrendered, snuggling comfortably into position against the solid bulk of Luke, imprisoned in the blatantly possessive circle of his arms.

'Can't offer you anything stronger than tea, coffee or fruit drinks. What shall it be? Coffee? Splendid! Madho?' The servant popped out of the shadows and was given instructions in a spate of Hindustani. Having disposed of this gesture of hospitality, the stout little hostess plumped herself in the camp chair next to Selina with a satisfied: 'Ah-h-h!'

The group began conversing and to forestall questioning Selina took the initiative. 'You speak the language beautifully, Mrs Martin. Have you been in India long?' she asked her neighbour politely.

'Longer than *you've* lived, my dear,' was the

cheerful reply. 'My husband's a doctor, you know. Thirty years in the medical missions. Too old to adapt to the English climate again, so we decided to retire here. We spend the winter months in Lucknow. On the plains—historic old place, you ought to visit it. In summer our home is here in the hills near Almora. Did you come through Almora, by any chance?'

Careful! thought Selina. 'No, it was another way. I'm not sure....'

'Keeping away from towns, you lovebirds! Quite right too. Where will you be living after the honeymoon?'

Selina glanced at Luke, but he was discussing cameras with the tubby bearded Australian. She said as confidently as she could: 'Delhi, I suppose, or wherever my—my husband takes me.'

'Oh, Delhi. Pshew! Like a furnace in the hot weather and monsoon. Come and stay with us in Almora for a while if you find it too much. Open house, you know. Jai and Greta,' she looked towards the Indian zoologist and his lint-haired Danish wife talking to Dr Martin and Narayan on the other side of the fire, 'had to make this trip for the survey on tigers. Rather early in the season for us, but we offered to open up our house for their use. Thought we'd put on our hiking boots and keep them company. When you're retired,' she added crisply, 'the best way to kill time is to work it to death!'

Selina laughed obligingly at this pithy old maxim, and as the servant had arrived with coffee, she hoped her well-meaning hostess would forget about the invitation to Almora. However, as soon as she had made sure everyone had been served, she sat down

again, stirred her mug energetically and said:
'Remember, now. Any time you need a break from
the heat you must come to Briar Brae. That's the
name of our house. Just drop me a line.'

'It's very generous of you, but——'

'Can't even face the prospect of tearing yourself
away from him yet, eh?' she interposed waggishly.
'You'll have to, some time or other, you know!'

This was so true; so poignant a reminder of her
real plight, that Selina was startled into spilling her
coffee. Luke jerked upright sharply: 'Hey! What
gives, honey? That was hot!' She looked stricken,
stripped of pretence. She fumbled for a handkerchief and rubbed ineffectually at the stain on his
trouser leg, stopping short as she became conscious
of the taut, muscular thigh beneath.

She was trembling, and Luke said urgently:
'*Liefje?* What is it?'

'Nothing ... nothing. Luke, I'm sorry....'

'Bless my soul!' The woman looked puzzled and
disconcerted. 'My fault,' she said quickly in a bracing tone. 'Teasing your wife, Dr van Meer. The
very idea of parting from you for a short stay in
Almora upset her. Lucky man with such a sensitive
young bride—treasure her! Girls these days are
mostly hard as nails, and independent. Makes such a
delightful change.' She removed Selina's mug. 'I'll
get you some more coffee, my dear.'

'No—thank you, I'm fine. It doesn't matter
really,' Selina refused huskily, embarrassed by the
flattery which had come rattling out in an attempt
to smooth things over. She must think I'm soft in the
head! was her wry thought.

Luke drew her back once more. Mrs Martin

bustled about replenishing other coffee mugs, and under cover of renewed conversation Luke bent his head and whispered with a hint of laughter: 'Getting tricky, was it? Well, you spiked her guns, but did you have to scald the skin off me to do it?'

'I didn't mean to. . . .' She was still disturbed out of all proportion to a trivial accident, and hoped fervently that Luke hadn't heard the remark that precipitated it and guessed the real reason. 'I was flustered,' she confided lamely.

'Poor, *sensitive* little bride,' he mouthed mockingly, his warm, laughing breath tickling her ear and sending a shiver down her spine. She made an involuntary movement in response and felt his body stiffen and his arm contract like a band of tensile steel that almost crushed her ribs. His hand slid beneath the folds of her sheepskin jacket, lingered at her waist, then curved under her breast against the accelerating beat of her heart.

Selina stared up at him, bemused and wordless. The humour had suddenly vanished. His eyes were half shut, heavy lidded, and there were tight lines around his mouth. Her own eyes widened and darkened until she took a fluttering breath and dropped her gaze. Luke shifted abruptly away from her, putting space between them and draping his arm loosely round her shoulders.

'How's the survey going?' he called across the others to the Indian zoologist, his face an expressionless, coppery mask in the firelight.

Baffled by Luke's moods which seemed to keep her on a knife-edge of emotional uncertainty, Selina fumbled with the damp handkerchief and made a business of pushing it into her pocket. The wretched 'visit' was becoming a torment! Luke had the confidence to play this game, but those few unguarded seconds had so unnerved her that she sat like a puppet and made no further effort to converse. Mrs Martin eyed her quizzically once or twice, but she pretended to be keenly interested in what the zoologist was saying and presently found her attention caught.

'... an estimate in 1972 that there were fewer than eighteen hundred tigers left in India caused much concern and "Project Tiger" was started.'

'With international support?' Luke asked.

'It would not have been possible without. There was a five-year budget of forty million rupees, with a liberal contribution from the World Wildlife Fund. Since then there has certainly been some improvement, but not satisfactory. Changes are being made in the protected regions, patrols for poachers, and so on and so forth, and we must compile more accurate figures of the tiger population.'

'How do you keep track of them?'

'Difficult with animals in the wild, especially in thick jungle areas. Tigers go singly or in pairs and can range many miles for their prey. We follow up all information. We had news that a tiger had been heard calling in this district—not noted before. Now we have located it lying up in a cave some twenty miles down river from here; a fine healthy specimen. The pug-marks indicate ten feet in size. By the sound of his call he is hunting for a female, so we are hopeful of natural mating and cubs here.'

'Luke!' Selina became animated again. 'Do you think *we* might see ...?'

'We might,' he grinned, 'if you don't take fright. Narayan?'

'We can try, if you wish,' he agreed, smiling.

'What if we come face to face with it!' she shivered in anticipation.

The zoologist laughed: 'Shout, dear lady, and you'll drive him away!' and then, satisfied that they would use nothing more lethal than a camera, he gave them directions for finding possible places for a sighting.

A short while afterwards Luke signalled Narayan and the party broke up. Luke helped Selina to her feet and drew her arm through his. Patch, relegated firmly to the background on a lead with Kunwar Singh for the past hour, barked excitedly to be free, and as soon as he was released sniffed and snuffled assiduously around every item of gear in the strangers' camp, to the amusement of everyone except Luke who kept a sharp eye on the dog's antics. Patch's inquisitive nose! I owe my life to it, Selina thought.

Goodbyes and hopes of meeting again were said. Handshakes and addresses exchanged—bogus addresses as far as Luke and Narayan were concerned, Selina felt sure, suppressing an almost hysterical desire to giggle. The strain of keeping up appearances was beginning to tell, and she was impatient to get away to the comparative security of their own camp.

Kunwar brought the lantern and Luke whistled up the dog, and they strolled back in silence along the river track. Selina slipped her arm out of Luke's as soon as their camp fire came in sight. It was a beautiful night, full of the smell and sound of billowing water, with the moon floating like an ivory disc above the gorge.

Yes, it was beautiful—Selina sighed, mesmerised by the contrast of dense black shadow and bleached limestone, the eerie shapes of stunted trees and bushes clinging to ledges and crannies in the towering walls, humped boulders as white as alabaster and reflected moonlight running like veins of silver down the river bed.

Remote and mysterious, and as lonely as a crater on the moon.

CHAPTER NINE

Now that the visit was over, without any glaring blunders, Selina should have been able to relax, but she felt thoroughly unsettled. Reaction had set in.

The brooding scowl between Luke's brows as they returned to the fire, his dismissive: 'Goodnight, Selly,' when she stood irresolutely beside him for a moment, made her flinch. He lighted a cigarette and joined Narayan—inevitably—to discuss their impressions, and she got ready for bed, packed away her good clothes and crept under the blankets.

She tried to sleep, but her brain was too active, fretted with notions about herself and about Luke which had never troubled her before. As she fidgeted and tossed on the camp-cot, her mind went back to her childhood, her girlhood, to the agonising months with Henry and Delia and the obscure outlook ahead and she was filled with a terrible sense of isolation and heartbreak.

Luke came into the tent some time later. Selina was vibrantly aware of his presence moving quietly, getting down to his sleeping-bag. She lay with her head averted and eyes shut, striving to keep very still and breathe evenly, but wakefulness and unhappiness were slowly tearing her apart. Into the silence came the thin, lilting notes of a flute; a mere thread of sound echoing down the gorge from one of the hill men in the distant camp. It was sweet, plaintive *pahari* music, and the mournful cadences were the final straw. She buried her head in the pillow, stifling a moan.

'Selina?' Luke's hand came up and touched her shoulder. She turned towards him with another muffled groan. His hand stroked the hot flush on her cheek as he said, very gently: 'Sick or worried, or just feeling blue?'

'I can't sleep....' She gulped. 'I've been thinking ... my whole life's been a *mess* ... and it's become such a tangle now, I don't know what I'll do.'

There was a momentary silence. Luke said softly: 'We'll sort out the tangle, Selly, we'll work it out between us later. But the other problem, before we met—you called it a nightmare once.' His fingers sought her hand and enclosed it in a strong, warm grip. 'Trust me. Tell me about it.'

She rubbed the back of her other hand over her eyes. 'Sometimes it seems unreal now, as if it happened to someone else, but I can't get it out of my mind.' A quivering sigh. 'You won't believe me, nobody else did.'

'Try me,' he said, as he had said once before, but this time gently.

She sighed again. 'I was so happy as a baby. We have a four-hundred-year-old estate on the south coast of England, right down to the sea, and a big, rambling Elizabethan manor house. I loved that old house. It was beautiful—it still is....' She shifted restlessly, swallowing jerkily. 'My mother died when I was about six ... and it had an awful effect on my father. Oh, he was fond of me in his own way, I suppose, but he wasn't very good with children and my old nurse looked after me. I'm not sure how Father met Delia, she just moved in as a sort of

secretary, and to act as hostess for the business
tycoons and their wives he used to entertain at week-
ends. She was sweetness itself to me at first ... she's
petite and pretty and looks like a china doll. I was
only seven or eight, but I could see Father was—
well, infatuated. In a few months he married her
and everything changed....' Her voice faded.

'How, *liefje*?' he urged in a low, tender tone.

'Delia was smooth as honey when Father was
there, but behind his back she was cruel and spiteful
... I realise now that she already had ambitious
ideas, and I was in the way. She used to slap and
knock me about. Once she switched me mercilessly
on my bare legs with a riding crop. Abbey, my
nurse, was up in arms and threatened to go to my
father, but Delia soon fixed that. She blamed Abbey
for the state I was in ... said she had beaten me,
and was old and cantankerous and incompetent,
and had her dismissed.' She took a shaky breath,
remembering. 'After that it became hell. Delia was
clever enough not to batter me again, but ...' her
voice faltered, 'there are other ways of terrorising a
child ... locking me up for hours in a musty box-
room because she knew I was frightened of spiders
... starving me as *discipline* ... shouting ... burning
me with the tip of her cigarette and passing it off as
a childish hurt if my teacher at the local school
remarked on it.'

'My God! No one spoke up?' Luke's grip hardened with rising anger. 'Was your father so insensate
that he didn't know what was going on?'

'I can't blame him, Luke. He was frequently away
on business, and Delia had gradually brought in
all her own servants who turned a blind eye. I—I

think it must have been the beginning of Father's illness too. Anyway, it was bliss when I went to boarding school. That taught me poise and pride, the courage to brazen it out and defy Delia—though I still dreaded the holidays. By the time I was sixteen she couldn't touch me any more. I kept to myself and treated her with contempt. I played her own game: nice to her in front of my father but very insolent and unco-operative away from him.'

She put a hand over her eyes: 'Then Henry arrived—he's Delia's brother. Father was tragically ill and he came to manage the estate. Oh, God! ... from the start he pestered me, watching me like—like a loathsome snake, trying to fondle me whenever he could,' she shuddered. 'It got so bad I was afraid to be in the house with him. One day I was so keyed-up, I blurted out the whole miserable truth to my father even though he was too sick to do anything. But he must have had suspicions for a long time that they were plotting to take everything he had, and after he died there was a ghastly scene when the will was read. Delia got the minimum she was entitled to as his widow, and he left everything else to me, tied up till I'm of age or marry. And it all goes to the National Trust if I die unmarried.'

'Since then,' her clasp tightened convulsively on the tensed muscles of Luke's arm, 'they've tried every trick they know to get their hands on the estate. They were not very subtle about it either. For a month or two it was all sweetness and light—advising me about this marvellous plan to turn the estate over to developers, build a yacht marina in our bay, sell off the farms which have been in our family for generations, and convert our beautiful historic home into a hotel for tourists. All in my own interest for a secure, comfortable future—of course!' her lip curled bitterly.

'When that didn't work, they reverted to intimi-dation ... unmentionable things ... to get me to marry Henry, knowing they'd never get control of the property any other way.' She lay trembling. 'I *wouldn't* chicken out and run. I held on like grim death until I could oust them legally. They cut me off from my personal friends. They implied that I was delicate and unstable and had to be supervised. It was like being imprisoned. They were so *loving* and *generous* and *patient* with me in public that nobody would believe what they were up to! And with Henry there day in day out, I really began to look and behave like a nervous wreck. He suggested this holiday in the Reserve and ... oh! ... I imagined we'd be in a group, or at least with a guide, camping and moving around. When I found what it was really like ... isolated, shut in with them ... Luke, I couldn't ... *couldn't* take any more....' Her voice broke.

Having poured it all out, she began to weep, silently with deep, racking tremors that shook her whole body and washed away years of fear, loneliness and anguish.

Luke rose to his knees and lifted her against him, rocking her gently in his arms. 'It's all over now, Selly-girl, it's all over. You're still young and you have a lifetime to be happy and learn to forget the suffering. I'm sorry if I added to it with my crass assertions about your background, but I couldn't understand till you told me, could I?' His quiet voice went on murmuring soothingly in her ear until the weeping abated and she drew a shuddering breath.

'H-handkerchief?' she hiccuped. Luke searched for a tissue and waited as she blew her nose and wiped her blotched face. He stroked back the sticky hair from her forehead and lowered her back on to the pillow. Then he kissed her very gently on the lips and in the palm of her hand, and pulled the blankets over her.

She stared up at him, round-eyed, and he laughed softly and said: 'A few kisses are like a few tears— they do you good! Now close your eyes and relax.' And within a couple of seconds she was in a profound sleep.

The next morning Luke roused her well before daybreak, and they struck camp and set off down the gorge in starry darkness. 'Can't stomach socialising with that lot again!' he had grinned wryly as he put Selina up on the pony, glancing at the other camp upstream where there were no visible signs of life yet.

Selina took the pony over the uneven track carefully, but with a light heart. She felt as if she had shed a heavy weight overnight; and the best of it was that there was a distinct change in Luke's attitude towards her, an easy, friendly intimacy. She was glad all the misery and stress had spilled out of her, grateful that he had accepted the truth. Her affection for him shone in every glance, for she was too happy to try and hide it. The whole day passed in the same carefree mood. Her eyes sparkled, she was infused with energy and even managed to laugh naturally at his teasing references to Mrs Martin's encounter with his 'sensitive young bride'.

The men called a halt rather earlier than usual. The terrain had slowly changed as the high walls of the gorge declined and narrowed into forested ravines, then opened in a broad green river meadow basking in the late afternoon sunlight under the sheltering slopes and ridges of the surrounding hills. Luke and Narayan had chosen a grassy knoll on the spur of a hill, and Selina prodded the indefatigable little pony up the tufted grass to where the tents were being pitched and dismounted with a springy agility full of delight and high spirits.

Luke's eyes brimmed with benevolent amusement. 'Bright-eyed and bushy-tailed! That's what I like to see after a day's hard grind.'

'It isn't so hard now,' she tossed her head nonchalantly. 'Toffee takes the brunt of it.' She asked: 'Luke, what's the name of this lovely valley?' and he told her it was called Paharpani, meaning Mountain Water.

Below them the river ran along a rocky bed bridged by a rough structure of planks. On either side were fields of burgeoning crops irrigated by wooden runnels, and small groves of apple and pear trees misted over with blossom. Pathways crisscrossed the valley and led up past a fan of cultivated terraces to the village, shaded by ancient fig and walnut trees, on the south face of the hill opposite. Four women were washing clothes by an outcrop of boulders near the bridge, and further downstream lean, bony cattle were grazing on patches of scrub, and muddy black water-buffaloes stood in the shallows flicking their tails indolently at flies and midges. Over the valley came the faint tinkle of bells from a flock of goats being herded home, and for a second Selina saw a flash of blue-green iridescence as a kingfisher swooped down to the river bank.

She thought she had never been so happy in her life as they sat companionably by the fire that evening in the flush of sunset. Cloud shadows sailed across the valley and merged into purpling twilight, and from the dark doorways of the village fires and oil lamps fluttered dimly. Patch crouched beside her as usual, nose twitching as they ate their meal, patiently waiting his turn to be fed, but the hill-bred Toffee could forage for himself and was further up the hillside munching steadily at a bed of nettles.

Selina was so much at ease with the men now that during a lull in their conversation about Indian politics (of which she knew less than nothing) she ventured to lean against the brawny arm next to her.

'Luke, are you really'—she drawled it impishly —'Dr Lucas van Meer?'

His brows rose as he slanted a glance at her, then he said casually: 'What I told our friends last night is true. I'm a pharmacologist.'

'Oh-h-h.' She paused, caught the gleam in his eye but continued boldly: 'Are you an American? Sometimes your accent is very marked.'

'Elephant's child!'

'What?'

'Full of *satiable curiosity*, like the Elephant's Child in Kipling's Just So stories. In other words, you're full of questions.'

She laughed but persisted: 'You know all about me, but I know so little about you.'

'I reckon cosmopolitan would maybe suit me. The story goes that the van Meers emigrated from Holland to the Dutch colony, where New York is now, in the seventeenth century. We traded weapons to the Iroquois tribes in their wars with the Algonquin tribes and the French, and eventually moved over the New York frontier and across the St Lawrence.' He smiled mockingly. 'We don't go much on family trees, like you English, but my grandmother used to treasure a few relics and stories about our Dutch descent. I was born in Canada of a Dutch–Irish–French father and a Scottish mother. I went to college in Edinburgh. And I've lived and worked in London, New York, Rome, Bangkok, Hong Kong and a good many other places on the globe. So I guess you could say I'm a heterogeneous feller.'

Tongue-in-cheek, she said: 'You mean a mongrel —like Patch.' She threw back her head, tilted the tip of her nose upwards with her forefinger and added in a haughty, high-pitched voice: 'My go-o-ood man! you're absolutely beyond the pale!'

'And for that piece of insolence, Miss Roxley,' he threatened, 'you could get a go-o-ood tanning on your rear!'

'Promises, promises!' she gave a peal of laughter, looked up at him and felt her heart skip a beat at the tender laughter in his eyes. She looked away, colour staining her cheeks. She was exhilarated yet suddenly shy and turned to Narayan, only to find that he was chuckling quietly too.

She heard the click of Luke's lighter, smelt the smoke of his cigarette. She longed to glance at him again, but that sudden awareness remained, and to gain time she focused determinedly on the *paan* box

Narayan had produced. He seemed amused by her belated interest as she asked awkwardly: 'What exactly is the leaf you eat, Mr Narayan?'

'Well. Here is the *paan*, a betel-pepper leaf. On it we spread shell lime—this white substance—thus. Then we fold the leaf into a small cone, thus. Put in a piece of areca nut and also a piece of gambier. And this we Indians chew, as you have seen, for a digestive and mild stimulant. I would offer it to you, Miss Roxley, but I fear you would find the taste too bitter and astringent, and it would stain your saliva with redness.'

Just at that moment Patch started to bark and a figure carrying a bundle and hurricane lantern climbed the slope into the camp, calling out as he came. The two men rose with alacrity, hailing him as Govind Singh, and immediately began a lengthy, confidential interrogation. It was clearly a pre-arranged meeting at this particular point of the trek.

Kunwar removed Patch to feed him, but the talk lasted so long that the dog had sneaked back and settled down beside Selina again before the newcomer was sent off with Kunwar to eat and rest. Luke and Narayan returned to the fire, took out a map and set up the lamps to study it.

Luke said: 'That guy's done a good job.'

'He is one of the best men I have. So then, we were right, eh? They came over the border from Nepal to Askot. Across the upper valley of the Ramganga River to Gangolihat.' The Indian's thin brown finger traced the line. 'North to Bhatgaon, and now travelling west to the river crossing at Bageshwar. That is where the change over and pay-off will take place.'

Luke bent over the map. 'Okay, the plan stands. We intercept them here,' he stabbed at the paper. 'There's no other way round, is there?'

'No, there is no other track between Bhatgaon and Bageshwar.'

Selina knew a moment's piercing disquiet, but in her present frame of mind she was able to suppress it. This was the mysterious rendezvous, the final purpose of their expedition—yet they sounded so matter-of-fact, supremely confident of handling it. And she had Luke's assurances about the future and trusted him. She sat quietly, her arm resting around the dog, until they had made their decisions about routes and distances.

When they began their preparations for the night, Patch was very reluctant to go to Kunwar. Selina stooped over him, fondling his head, and asked: 'Can't he stay with us, Luke? He could sleep under the camp-cot.'

'No, Selly, he's safer with Kunwar Singh. There are more leopards than tigers in the hills nowadays, and a leopard isn't above raiding for small domestic prey like dogs and chickens.'

She shivered. 'Then why did you bring him with you, for heaven's sake?'

'Well, I didn't risk his hide for the pleasure of his company,' he replied sardonically. 'He's useful.'

'*Useful?*'

'Yep, specially trained. Too useful to lose to a hungry leopard at this stage of the game.' He picked up the dog and handed him to Kunwar, and Selina knew he had no intention of explaining.

Puzzled and disappointed, she turned away, but Luke grasped her arm and brought her round to cup her face in his big hands. In the silent darkness they stood close together. His thumbs began to move gently over her cheeks and across the outline of her lips, and her vague sense of pique melted into a pulsing sweetness at his touch. Slowly he released her.

'Go to bed, *liefje*,' he said softly. 'And don't worry —about anything.'

Later, curled up on the camp-cot, she had fleeting thoughts about leopards and a good deal else, then drifted into a deep, dreamless sleep.

If the idea of leopards in the vicinity had troubled her the night before, the zoologist's tiger appeared as a living, breathing, terrifyingly beautiful reality the following day—an unplanned, unexpected sighting. Selina had been surprised after they crossed the river to find that they were heading back towards the mouth of the gorge, but it was not for her to question the change of direction. The pony was picking his surefooted way along the track through shady ravines of mixed oak, pine and rhododendron forest; birds sang in the trees and thickets, Patch was snug in the haversack on Luke's back, splashes of sunshine chequered the rough trail and poured like spotlights into the open glades. It was a warm tranquil morning.

The first warning came from *langur* monkeys. Selina could hear them in the trees and Luke pointed one out swinging nearby on low-slung branches. Unlike the small rhesus monkey, it was a long, slender, grey creature with narrow, dark nostrils, lanky legs and a very long tail. Suddenly it sheered off into the treetops and from further down the trail the whooping call of the rest of the troop altered to harsh, guttural cries of alarm.

At the head of the line Narayan, Govind Singh and the man who had been acting as guide halted. The mules had stopped instinctively, forelegs stiff and rumps tucked well down as they refused to move. Kunwar grabbed Toffee's bridle. Selina could feel the uneasy pony trembling in every limb. Soon not only the monkeys but the birds and the distant barking of a *kakar* deer were all sounding the alarm. Luke hauled Selina off the pony and drew her back so that he could see both up and down the trail, holding her in the kind of grip that could instantly pitch her one way or the other to safety. Listening to Patch's muffled whimpering, feeling Luke's unnatural stillness hard against her, watching the pony's eyes rolling, its nostrils flaring, Selina was dumb, paralysed with fright. She had never experienced such an acute sensation of hidden, stealthy menace in her life.

'*There,*' Luke whispered sharply. 'On the rocks in the gully.'

She didn't want to look, but her eyes were irresistibly drawn to a pile of broken rock some fifty yards ahead where the track dipped through a hollow. Whatever she had expected to see, it was not that great feline head upon powerful shoulders, moving slowly, regally as the tiger scanned the track from the top of a flat rock. The sun put a sheen on his broad back and loins: red-brown shading to fawn enhanced by a striking pattern of sinewy black transverse stripes that seemed to ripple over his muscles.

As if at a given signal, the men in front began to shout and bang sticks together, the mules started to kick wildly, loose tins and pans clanking on their packs, and in the shock of this hubbub the tiger growled, crouched and sprang with tremendous grace and strength high over the track and down into the thickets on the far side. A last angry flash of his long tail and he could be heard bounding away through the trees and undergrowth, arousing warning cries from other animals on the slope below.

Selina buried her face in her hands, shaking from head to foot. 'Hey now!' said a bracingly ironic voice in her ear. 'Who wanted to see Sher Bahadur free in his native land?'

'N-not s-suddenly like t-that. . . .'

'All laid on, ma'am, no trouble at all. Here, up you get.' Luke lifted her back into the saddle. 'Okay?' he called to Narayan. The Indian responded. The pony had calmed down with Kunwar's firm hand on the bridle, but it took another minute or two for the hill men to bring their mules under control.

'You didn't get a photograph,' Selina succeeded in joking weakly.

'I had other things on my mind. You for a start.' Luke's clear grey eyes held hers. 'He was a fine young male, Selly, healthy and strong enough to go after his natural prey. They seldom attack unless they're cornered or harassed, or a tigress protecting cubs. But sometimes if they're wounded or too old to hunt they'll kill humans because humans are easy prey, and it makes sense to be wary of any animal in the wild. Savvy?'

She nodded. She was still strung up, clutching the reins tightly as they moved on at a faster pace. About an hour later they caught a distant sound, a faint moaning roar fluctuating on the breeze so far behind them that her jittery nerves began to settle down. When they halted at midday Narayan confirmed that they were beyond the tiger's usual territory, and by nightfall she had forgotten her terror and remembered only the superb arrogance, vigour and rich, flowing colouration of the jungle monarch.

Selina's mind returned to this indelible image many times in the next day or so as they trekked over the heights beyond the gorge; then it was temporarily lost in the qualms and exertions of the longest, most dangerous climb she had yet been required to tackle. The trail was little more than an old, ill-defined goat-path zigzagging in tortuous bends across the bare shoulder of an escarpment, and gazing at the almost perpendicular ascent she couldn't conceal her dismay.

The leaders set off, carefully choosing and testing their footholds. The mules were taken by cautious stages up each rugged section. Selina closed her eyes and tried to shut her ears to the clatter of rubble bouncing down the *khud*. Kunwar was at the pony's head, Luke brought up the rear. She kept telling herself she had nothing to fear, but she felt sick stooping forward over the pommel, pinched and chafed by the saddle with every jolt upwards. As Kunwar eased the gallant little pony around a bend she opened her eyes for a second and her head reeled to see a sheer drop on the other side where a landslide had cut a massive swathe of scarred earth, rocks, battered trees and other debris down the mountain.

'Luke ...' she wailed, 'I can't ... I can't!'

'You can,' he shouted impatiently, and she squeezed her eyelids tight together as the pony jerked into motion again.

Presently they reached a shelf of projecting rock about six feet wide. Luke called to Kunwar and they halted. He edged alongside and lifted Selina off the saddle, taking her round the back of the pony with him.

'Here, get hold of this and hang on.' He gathered up the pony's tail and put it into her clammy, tremulous hands. 'Grip hard, Selina, let him take the strain without weight, and I'll be right behind you.'

In this way they completed the climb in an amazingly short time: Kunwar Singh leading and encouraging the pony, Selina clinging to the end of the tail as though it were a tow-rope pulling her upwards, and Luke close on her heels giving her an occasional push, exhorting her to: 'Go on, go on. You're going to make it, girl, you're going to make it!'

She was concentrating so hard on her feet and her grip on Toffee's tail that she forgot her fears and could scarcely believe it when the path levelled out all of a sudden and the pull of the tail slacked off. She looked up dizzily. They were on a ridge below a meadow blobbed with thawing snow and clusters of mountain primroses, sloping uphill into a soaring pine forest. She was gasping in the cold air, her knees wobbling with strain, her palms red and slightly sore. She all but collapsed against Luke.

Supporting her with one arm, Luke removed her hat, ran his fingers through her damp hair and pressed her head into his chest. She could hear the quickened thud of his heart beating into her, and a feeling of intensely physical affection shot through her entire body. Moving very slowly, she released

her arms and slid them round him. He tilted her
face back and bent to put his lips against the curve
of her throat and murmur huskily: 'It's all right,
liefje. You were great. It's all over now, sweetheart.'

Selina's clasp tightened convulsively. She couldn't
get close enough. A wave of poignant longing raced
through her veins, pounding in her head, pulsating
under her ribs until she couldn't contain it any
longer.

Words tumbled from her lips in an ardent
whisper: 'Luke ... I ... I love you. I love you so!
I'd do anything to please you....'

He raised his head, met her eyes and saw this
passionate avowal reflected in the very dark, limpid
violet depths. His own eyes had an arrested look
which held and dominated hers for so long that
her mind became a whirling blank in which her
only consciousness was of the physical contact and
tension between them. Luke's gaze became heavy-
lidded. Lines appeared around his mouth and nostrils. His encircling arms grew taut and began to
crush her slim body as if he was unaware of the force
he was exerting. The pain of it drew a stifled cry
from her, and his arms unlocked at once. Loosen-
ing her clasp from around his waist, he thrust her
away from him.

'Anything?' he said in a deliberately cynical, offhand tone. 'That's a rash offer I can do without, you
little fool,' and he picked up her hat.

The rejection was more than she could bear. She
swung round and walked away towards where Kunwar stood discreetly by the pony, fighting to salvage
some of her self-respect. She looped an arm about the
pony's neck and stroked and patted him, her throat

jerking as she swallowed tears welling up from a ferment of emotions and a feeling of humiliation not even Henry could have inflicted on her. She struggled to find a light or caustic retort, but it was beyond her. Mounting the pony, she kicked him into a trot along the ridge in the direction the others had gone, leaving Luke and his servant without a backward glance.

A grievous estrangement followed. Selina's mortification was like a raw wound, hurting as much from the sudden discovery of her real feelings for him as from his rebuff. The big brush-off! she thought numbly when Luke quietly extracted his gear and sleeping-bag from her tent and thereafter trekked with the Indians. She must have been out of her mind, offering him her love like that; out of her subconscious mind—that was where it had come from, unbidden. And embarrassingly unwelcome as far as he was concerned.

Blame it on folly and inexperience. She had mistaken Luke's gentler protective impulses, opened her hungry heart and artlessly assumed her growing love for him was merely affection. The most bitter irony of her unhappy life, she thought wearily, was loathing Henry who had never ceased wanting her, pestering her; and falling in love with Luke who didn't find her physically attractive. Luke had been as kind, reassuring and sympathetic as a really close friend but, thinking back, she could see that he had always shied at the first sign of any explicit emotional response towards him.

And now she couldn't even talk to him except for the occasional word about essentials when camping. Kunwar Singh seemed to have taken over re-

sponsibility for her welfare, and although the old
servant was fatherly and attentive, Selina felt as if
a part of her had gone over that awesome cliff and
died.

They left the high pines for chestnut and oak
woods again, which suited Toffee. The pony relished
oak leaves cut down for him to feed on; but there
were other denizens of these woods who liked rooting in the brush for caches of nuts and acorns. Selina
spotted two of them grunting and threshing about
in a quarrel on the slope above the camp, and stood
quite still, towel in hand, while a pair of small
Himalayan black bears, scarcely five feet tall on
their hindlegs and with that distinctive V of white
fur on their chests, took a few angry swipes at each
other, then ambled off the opposite way from the
stream she was using.

Uncaring to the point of carelessness, she had not
been particularly scared, nor interested enough to
mention it at the evening meal. The constraint at
the fireside was almost tangible, and if she had not
been so numbed and apathetic she would have de-
tected subtler tensions. Both men were on edge,
silent and preoccupied. As soon as they had eaten
they went to Narayan's tent where they were joined
by Govind Singh and the guide, and Selina could
hear the muted rumble of their deliberations far
into the night.

But she no longer cared about the trek, or what
would become of her.

CHAPTER TEN

By morning things had changed inexplicably. There was no sign of Luke and Narayan when Selina emerged from her tent, and although the other men were going about their tasks in the ordinary way, there was a strange, hushed atmosphere in the camp which penetrated her dull indifference and filled her with an uneasy sense of premonition.

Pale and heavy-eyed, she sat by the camp fire sipping tea Kunwar had made for her and watched the loads being packed. Patch crouched at her feet, whimpering occasionally as if he, too, sensed her foreboding.

'Where is . . . where are the *sahibs*?' she enquired hesitantly.

'They are going off early,' the old servant informed her. 'But not to worry. They are coming back soon in the daytime.'

She poured what was left of the tea into a pan for Patch to lap up. Kunwar asked her about breakfast; she thanked him politely but refused. The very thought of food at the moment turned her stomach with aversion. He clicked his tongue in disapproval and tried persuasion, but Selina was adamant about not wanting to eat.

While she went for a wash, Kunwar Singh packed for her and had the tents dismantled. Afterwards, as she paced restlessly with nothing to do to take her mind off her uneasiness, she noticed that Govind

Singh and the guide had also disappeared. She wondered who would return to give instructions for moving on, and how long it would be. Patch added to her unsettled state of mind by following her around, snuffling at her heels, until she was inclined to get impatient with him.

When everything had been cleared, Selina suddenly discovered that Kunwar hadn't saddled Toffee, and the pony was being led away, off the track and around the back of the hill, along with the loaded mules.

'Stop!' she cried sharply. 'Where are they taking them?'

'Nothing to fear,' Kunwar assured her earnestly. 'The *sahib* has ordered it. I am going with the *memsahib* also. Another camp.'

'But why have they taken the pony away?' her voice rose uncertainly. 'Where is this—this other place?'

'A short walk only. More better for us to be on the other side,' he said placatingly. 'The *memsahib* is ready now?'

'No! ... oh, I don't know!' running her fingers agitatedly through her hair. 'Why didn't they leave a message for me?' she demanded plaintively, convinced that Luke had finally deserted her. They had gone to their secret rendezvous! It was happening now—only God knew where and what for—and she had been discarded with the rest of the baggage.

As if to confirm her apprehension the servant said: 'Both *sahibs* are having much business to arrange. The Doctor *sahib* was not liking to disturb your sleep, but he gave me *hukkum*, that is very especial order to see you are all right.'

Selina closed her eyes for a second and took a steadying breath. She had no alternative but to accompany him. 'Very well,' she sighed heavily, and followed him slowly across the slope and through the trees.

It was rough terrain and Selina picked up the dog to prevent his straying. The trail was little more than broken bushes and crushed undergrowth where the muleteers had passed, to which Kunwar added a few identifying marks by cutting notches in trees with a penknife. Selina scrambled along behind the servant. After about ten minutes of hard going she began to tire, her eyes glazing as a feeling of helplessness sapped what little energy she had.

She was about to tell Kunwar she would have to take a rest when they came into a small glen hidden among the trees with a stream leaping down stones at the bottom. In a clearing on one side of this gully all the gear and stores had been unloaded and the tents set up again. The sight rallied her spirits a little until she looked across the stream; Toffee and the mules were cropping the grass contentedly, but further down a group of about six men Selina had never seen before had bivouacked around a camp fire of their own. They were as shabbily dressed as the hill men and looked frighteningly like bandits as they squatted under the trees holding long, knotted sticks like cudgels, every brown face staring balefully at her.

The dog struggled out of her arms and raced off to bark at them from the edge of the water. Selina spun round towards the servant in a panic, knowing the old man wouldn't be able to protect her from these ruffians, thinking for wild seconds that he might purposely have led her into a trap.

'Nothing to fear,' Kunwar pacified her hastily,
'No, no. Nothing to fear. They are Narayan *sahib*'s
men. Take repose by the tent, *memsahib*, I will
make you a cool drink.' He went down to call the
dog and had a brief word with the men, and when
Selina had summoned the courage to have another
look at them they were smiling and exchanging
jokes. The expressions she had imagined baleful
were probably just curious. Nevertheless she was
still worried by their appearance, and wary, and sat
down where she could keep an eye on them.

She gulped the fruit drink thirstily but continued to refuse any food, and having failed to coax
her, the servant threw up his hands. '*Thoba-thoba*!
Luke *sahib* will beat me for this,' he mourned jest-
ingly. 'I am dismissed!'

Luke wouldn't know; and would he still care
if he did? Selina thought wanly. 'Why have we
moved to this camp with those men?' her voice
shook.

Kunwar paused and then as if he realised the
strain she was suffering said quietly: 'It is a good
place, far from the road where is Bhutia's place, and
no sound of us is reaching there. These extra men
are coming from Ranikhet by another road. To
everyone they are only hill travellers, but the *sahibs*
have need of them.'

Selina's earliest misgivings, that Luke and Narayan were involved in something dangerous, surfaced
again filling her with dread.

'What is a—a Bhutia?'

'A man from Bhutan state. How can I explaining it to *memsahib*....' he rubbed his grizzled chin.

'There is Indian hill people, and there is other mountain people. Different from us—like Tibetan kind of people. They are from Nepal, Sikkim and Bhutan. This Bhutia is trader here for salt, flour *gûr* and other things. His place is by the pass where travellers are stopping to buy food. Some bad men stopping there now,' he concluded, wagging his head and clicking his tongue, unaware that he was adding to Selina's dread.

Wordlessly, she nodded as though she understood, but her thoughts were spinning with the ominous implications of what he had said. Two points seemed clear: there was going to be a confrontation between Luke and Narayan and the 'bad men', as Kunwar naïvely expressed it; and since reinforcements with cudgels had arrived secretly, and the camp was carefully hidden at the back of the hill, it was to be a surprise attack. And soon; any time soon.

So, where was Luke now? she cried silently. Planning the attack. She had never met organised violence before—not the lethal violence of men against men, with weapons. She shuddered, wrapping her arms about herself and rocking to and fro to relieve her stress. At least he would be returning to the camp, as Kunwar had told her first thing in the morning. At least she would be seeing him again. All Luke's warnings about secrecy and safety crowded in on her as she watched the tree shadows change, moving imperceptibly with the sunlight as the hours passed.

Then suddenly he was there, with no more than the snap of a twig and Patch darting away from her. In spite of his husky size he had arrived as stealthily

as the tiger through the forest. Selina rose stiffly
from a box she was sitting on and faced him, her
heart thumping. She wanted to run and throw
herself into his arms, but her legs wouldn't move.
She stood with her fingers pressed over her mouth,
her gaze revealing more than she realised.

Luke closed the gap in a couple of strides and
stared at her pinched face. 'Selina?' he scowled.
'Are you all right? You look ill.'

She was floundering in a stormy whirl of mingled
relief and love for him, and consuming anxiety.
'Why ... why are you d-doing this?' she burst out
in an agonised voice.

'What am I supposed to be doing to warrant that
reproachful tone?'

'Fighting ... killing, perhaps....'

The grey eyes sharpened into flints. 'Because it
has to be done. You knew from the start we had a
tough job to do. And this is it.'

'What is it? What?' she exclaimed desperately,
her voice rising hysterically. 'I wish to God I could
understand what's happening, and why!'

Luke's hand shot out, grasped her wrist and
twisted her towards the tent. 'You're making a scene,
Selina. It's not good for morale. Get in there.' He
pushed through the tent flap and dumped her on
the camp-cot. She flinched away from him, rubbing
her wrist. Luke had reverted to the stranger she had
first met—hard, ruthless and sardonic. And in her
present state she couldn't combat his rough domin-
ance.

'Listen to me. I guess you can take it now.' He
went down on his heels by the tent flap, his large
frame a solid barrier against the men outside. 'I'm

an agent for an international bureau whose job is to crack down on the gangs trading in narcotics. Do you know what I mean?'

She drew in her breath. 'Drugs?' she whispered, her eyes dilating.

'Yep. This is a drugs bust, Selina.'

'Here?' There was shock and bewilderment in her gaze. 'At the back of beyond? But what could they do with it here?'

He laughed; a harsh, humourless sound. 'They'll try any route and the most ingenious and sometimes incredible methods to get the junk on to the big markets. It's an industry, Selly, a multi-million-dollar business.' He shifted and sat on the camp-cot beside her, taking her hands in his. 'Have you heard of the Golden Triangle?'

She shook her head mutely. He said: 'It's a remote region in the hills on the borders of Burma and Thailand. Poverty-stricken farmers grow crops of poppies and harvest hundreds of tons of raw opium in an area so isolated the authorities can't police it. Traders—mostly brigands and rival guerilla armies fighting to take control—collect the opium and deliver it to secret refineries where they manufacture illicit morphine, and the drug which causes so much misery and death—heroin, a derivative of morphine.

'Then the criminal syndicates take over.' Selina could feel the anger building up in him. 'Groups like the Chinese Triad secret societies and other vicious gangs of wholesale brokers and traffickers. They smuggle it across oceans and continents, through stages of couriers, until it gets down to the local pushers to sell to pitifully desperate junkies

who go on paying higher and higher prices for a
fix. By which time the deadly muck has often been
adulterated with talcum or milk powder or other
substances to boost profits. God! When I think of
the money which could be spent every year on
fighting disease, famine and poverty all over the
world, going into the hands of——'

He broke off, his grip so tight now that Selina felt
the bones in her fingers would crack. Despite the
pain, she stayed quite motionless and prompted
softly: 'And *this* job ... how did you know it was
going on here?'

'Narcotics intelligence.' His grip eased slightly.
'Every time we arrest couriers, uncover their
methods and routes, break up gangs, they recruit
others and find new ways of smuggling. We can't
always beat the bastards, but European, Asian and
American drug squads are combining to keep each
other posted on the identity of traffickers and the
routes and techniques they're using and when we
catch 'em at it, it isn't just making a haul but saving
the lives of potential addicts. Every little counts,
Selly.'

She wriggled her hands free and turned them
over, changing his grip to a clasp between them. He
looked out beyond the tent flap to where the Indians
were standing respectfully, almost to attention, obviously receiving final instructions from Narayan in
the fading light.

'Narayan and I,' he continued, 'and a Nepalese
officer, Bala Sen, met up a few years ago at a conference of policemen from eighteen countries held
at Chiang Mai, in Thailand.' He looked down at
Selina. 'Two years back Bala Sen had a tip-off that a

syndicate was using the tourist trade to Nepal to smuggle in junk. When a substantial supply had been delivered by couriers it was being sent by mule convoys over the border into India and along the Himalayan back trails to Kashmir and Jammu, then across the Afghan frontier for distribution. We hadn't a hope in hell of nailing them once a shipment was split up again; it had to be somewhere en route. And this is it, Selly, this particular buck stops here. It's taken us months checking it out and setting it up, working under cover.'

Luke's crusade! she thought, curling her fingers closer around his.

'And then I nearly ruined it for you at the last moment. Oh, Luke ... I was only thinking of myself ... I wish I'd known,' she murmured huskily.

'How could you?' he said wryly. 'We might have got you away to England if Spender hadn't kicked up enough publicity to blow the whole operation. It was a hell of a decision we had to make!' His jaw flexed grimly. 'We put you through it, Selly, and you've done better than we reckoned. These drug runners aren't in it for peanuts, you know. They'd slit a few throats, or use torture, on the slightest pretext. If you'd had any notion of the facts—if you'd fallen into their hands—my God!——' he stopped abruptly.

The sun had set, and menacing shadows seemed to stalk the gully outside. Just as well she hadn't known before, she thought, shivering with horror as her imagination filled in what he had left unsaid.

He suddenly gathered her close. 'I've lost someone to them already. I'm not losing you.'

She lifted her head. 'I'm not losing you' sang

through her brain. Fixing her eyes on his face, she breathed: 'Who? Who did you lose, Luke?'

She felt his sigh warm on her face. 'My sister, Anna. She was a heroin addict at eighteen. She tried to kick the habit, but she wasn't strong enough. She took an overdose.' There was a taut silence. 'That's when I quit being a smart pharmacologist, lecturing medical students and working in spotlessly clean, expensively equipped laboratories, and became a policeman.' He jerked her away roughly. 'And that's why it makes me hopping mad to hear a young girl talking about suicide.'

As she had done in a fit of panic that day in the little car—now it came back to her with a rush of feeling. Luke's cold white rage about 'human predators', and the certainty she had had that the trek was more than just a job to him, almost a personal vendetta. It all began to fall into place: his edgy moods; the way he had watched over her; the smallest incidents of the days they had shared. Her heart swelled with love and tenderness.

She threw her arms around his neck, pressed her cheek to his. 'I'm sorry, Luke ... I'm sorry,' she whispered tremulously.

'Sorry we ever met?' he mocked gently. 'That figures!'

'No! ... no! Don't make fun of me now, Luke, I can't bear it....'

His hard, stubbled jaw caressed her temple and down her cheek rousing a sensation of physical excitement deep in the core of her being which spread along her nerves until she turned her head, with a small, muffled exclamation, and put her lips to his.

Luke tensed, and for a couple of seconds his

mouth was a hard, resistant line; then, as though something had snapped, he began kissing her. She was pinned against the muscular wall of his chest as he possessed her mouth with urgent intimacy, and Selina responded ardently in a fever of instinct and longing that emptied her mind of everything except her own need of him.

Narayan had spoken Luke's name twice before the sound penetrated their absorption. Luke dragged his mouth from hers and pulled her entwined arms from his neck. Outside, the glen was as dark as the tent and unnaturally quiet. Awareness of what lay ahead of Luke in the darkness on the other side of the hill flooded back to her, and she gasped a plea: 'Luke ... don't go. ...'

He pushed her aside, breathing heavily, and hastened out of the tent and down to the stream to splash water over his face and head. Selina could just make out the shadows of the men waiting under the trees. The camp fires were out, and the only glimmer came from a hurricane lantern. In its fitful beam she saw Narayan pass Luke a shoulder-holster, saw Luke strap it on. Still dazed, she felt she was in the middle of another nightmare.

She stumbled out of the tent as Luke returned and loomed over her. His eyes were glittering, his features a mask of scored lines, dark as ebony.

'You once said you'd do anything for me. Well, do it now,' he demanded in a terse undertone. 'Lie low and stay put, whatever happens. Unless you hear from me or Narayan. Do you understand?' Selina's horrified gaze was riveted on the black handle protruding from the holster. 'Did you hear what I said?' he rapped out harshly. 'We're leaving Kunwar Singh and the guide to guard you, and the muleteers will guard the animals and keep watch.'

'I'll look after Patch,' she entreated; Govind Singh had picked him up and was crossing the stream. 'I'll have him with me. I'll keep him quiet.'

'No. He goes with us. It may be a straightforward bust, but smugglers think up inventive gimmicks for concealing drugs in case there's trouble. Patch has been trained to sniff out junk. If it's there he'll locate it, no matter what.' Luke's hand lifted; dropped back to his side without touching her. 'We must leave now to get to the pass before the moon comes up. Stay in the tent, Selly, get your head down and try to sleep.'

He had a brusque last word with Kunwar Singh and the guide and, without giving her another glance, strode down the slope and across the stream. Selina watched the silent figures melting into the forest; the light from their lantern dwindling like a faint will-o'-the-wisp until it disappeared.

How long she stood staring blindly into the blackness, she never knew. She was shivering from head to foot. It was a bitterly cold night, she thought vaguely. She started and nearly cried out at the feel of something on her shoulders, then found that it was the servant draping a blanket round her.

'Not allowing fire. Not warm, and I cannot cook for the *memsahib*,' he said with sympathetic concern. '*Memsahib* go in tent now.'

'It's all right,' she responded dully. Cautiously, stumbling a little, she laved her face in the stream, and made use of a sheltering bush before returning to the tent to crouch on the camp-cot in a terrified stupor.

It was the longest night she had ever endured, every hour a lifetime fraught with suspense. The darkness was like a pall. The only sounds that reached her were restless movements from the pony and mules, the muted scratching and rustling of nocturnal forest creatures and occasional whispers of conversation from the two men guarding the tent. Her body was chilled to the bone, yet she had to wipe clammy perspiration from her palms and upper lip. When the sudden call of a night-bird startled her to her feet she felt giddy with stress, fatigue and lack of food, and lay down on the camp-cot and pulled the blankets well up over her shoulders and head. She closed her eyes on her anguished thoughts, her lips moving in a silent, repetitive prayer. Slowly, she slipped over the edge into oblivion.

A shaft of sunlight danced on Selina's eyelids, goading her into awareness until she sat bolt upright with a jerk. Still hazy with sleep, she noticed the tent flap wide open to a view of Kunwar sitting by the camp fire, the kettle steaming on the Primus stove, and Patch in the distance blithely lifting his leg against an oak tree.

Luke ... *Luke* ... Selina flung off the blankets, scrabbled for her shoes.

She almost fell over him as he lay in his sleeping-bag a few feet from the tent. Overcome with searing relief, she pressed a hand to the ache in her empty stomach, swayed on her feet and sank to her knees beside him, tears trickling down her face. One grey eye opened, squinting drowsily in the sunlight; then the other; then Luke's arms came up and drew her down to him. And the hard warmth of his shoulder, the rough tenderness of his fingers brushing away her tears, conveyed a glorious sense of reprieve. She released a long, quivering sigh: 'It's over ... and you're all right....'

'Mm-m.' He yawned hugely. 'Not a scratch to cry about.'

'Oh, thank God!' She turned her face into the hollow of his neck. It took her a long while to regain enough control to ask him about the raid.

'Our cover must have held well. No leaks, no suspicions. We caught them squarely on the hop.' He settled her more comfortably in his arm. 'They've had it so easy on other convoys that discipline had become slack. These guys are too wily to take drugs themselves, but they'd been passing a few jugs of native liquor around and were sleeping it off. Even the men on watch were dozy.' He yawned again himself. 'All over in ten minutes, barring some fractures and sore heads.' Selina shuddered at the laconic way he shrugged it off, and he added impatiently: 'Okay, okay. They're all alive, fit to travel and stand trial.'

'Where are they now?'

'Manacled and under guard on the bit of camp-ground by the Bhutia's hut near the pass. The couriers waiting to take over at Bageshwar will cool their heels for a day or two and then get the message! This is one route that won't be bringing in the big money again. Bala Sen will arrest the middle-men in Nepal as soon as we radio him the top names and the haul.'

'Was Mr Narayan hurt?'

'Nope. He's still on duty, in charge of the camp.

This is Indian territory, Narayan's jurisdiction. He has the legal authority to detain them. Looks like being the biggest ever haul to his credit, and he deserves it.'

'Looks like? Aren't you sure?'

'Not yet,' there was a thread of humour in his lazy tone. 'All that we found in the mule-packs were bales of cloth! That threw us for a while. But the dog wouldn't leave the packs alone, and we trust that scallywag's sensitive nose more than our own judgement. The old pharmacology came in handy there. It dawned on me that the heroin had been reduced to a paste, and the cloth impregnated with it. No telling how much the haul is worth till we retrieve the heroin from the cloth.'

'Heavens! I wouldn't have believed they were so—so crafty!'

'Cunning as a barrel of monkeys,' he agreed idly. Selina felt his chest rise and his muscles expand as he stretched luxuriously, and the effect was an immediate heightening of her senses to the vital masculinity beside her.

A small but fervid hope, kindled by the passionate way Luke had kissed her the night before, set her heart beating fast again. He was relaxed in mind and body after months of planning and activity. What better opportunity to gauge his true feelings than these precious moments together? He would be caught up in other plans, other preoccupations later on.

She approached it obliquely: 'Luke ... what happens now?'

'Taking the prisoners and that valuable cargo safely to Ranikhet, and fixing transportation to

Delhi,' he said, elaborately casual. 'Then we'll sort out Spender, if he's still around, and put you—unscathed!—on to a flight for England. I have friends in London you can go to. He's a lawyer, a good one. He and his wife will help you get things straight.'

'No!' she sat up sharply and wrapped her arms around her knees. Her mouth was dry. This was a crucial moment. 'I want to stay with you, Luke.'

'No way,' he shot back at her promptly as if he had expected it.

'Why not?' she implored, her voice wavering.

'Because gratitude isn't a good enough reason for tying yourself down when you're still so young.' She turned her head and gave him a speaking look, but his expression was hard. 'Oh, sure, you fancy yourself in love with me at the moment, but it won't last, Selina. It's just an outlet for the affection you've never had, and a reaction against Spender's greedy lechery,' he said bluntly.

She paused, stricken, resting her head on her knees. 'If that's all you think it is, why did you kiss me as though —as you did last night?'

'Oh, for God's sake! After all your experiences with Spender, don't you know anything about men?' He rubbed a hand over his eyes. 'Look, how do you think a man feels when he finds himself in the back-blocks with a desirable girl, night and day, for days on end! It's a compulsive natural instinct at the best of times, Selina, and under these conditions absolute self-control would take a miracle. And I'm no saint! Okay, so I succeeded up to a point—I had to move out of the tent and try to keep my distance when you became overwrought and things were getting out of hand. But last night was different. There were exceptional tensions; mutual tensions of a kind that don't arise in the ordinary way.'

She forced herself to speak, in bitter resignation: 'That's all it meant to you ... just propinquity, and an emotional girl adding complications to an already tricky situation.'

His lips twisted. 'I didn't say that.' He looked at the slender, forlorn figure hunched beside him, her pale, drawn face gazing down at him.

'Well, whatever you say, Luke, it meant a lot to me,' she told him gravely. 'I love you, and always will. You see, I know and understand what I want better than most girls my age because I've had years learning exactly what I *don't* want. The hard way. I need what only someone like you can give me—as a lover, and trusted friend. You've been all over the world and met lots of women, Luke, and if I'm not the type that appeals to you except in—well— certain circumstances. ...' She averted her head, and ended with quiet dignity: 'I'm sorry if I've embarrassed you.'

He groaned. 'It wouldn't work, Selly!' For the first time she heard a note of uncertainty in his usually decisive voice. 'You couldn't take the life I have to lead. Moving from pillar to post, without a settled home in any one place for long. Then there's the risk involved; as my wife you might become a target for goons with a grudge to work off against me.' He sat up. 'It's not on,' he said curtly, and glanced at her to find her round, limpid eyes fixed on him with dawning knowledge. 'Selly, *no*,' he emphasised roughly. 'And don't suggest that I give up this job. Because I'm not cut out to help you run your classy, old-world country estate in rural England!'

She swayed towards him, lips parted, eyes shining exultantly in her tear-stained, tired face. 'Who's asking you?' she said softly.

Luke looked deep into her eyes. 'Have you any idea what this is doing to me?' he said gruffly, and elation soared in her, making her heart race.

She smiled. 'Last night, when you kissed me ... that's the way you really feel about me, isn't it?' She could read the signs now in his taut features.

'Yes.' The muscle flexed in his tense jawline. 'Yes, you crazy, stubborn, imprudent little——' He seized her slim body in a bruising hold and tipped her backwards to the ground, crushing the breath out of her with the weight of his chest and his hungry mouth. Selina returned his kisses, moving her head restlessly, pliant in his hands, as deeply aroused as he was. Minutes later she suddenly felt something warm snuffling at her hair and went rigid.

Luke raised his head, breathing unevenly, and chuckled. 'Get out of here, you inquisitive pooch, this is private!' he roared, and Selina winced, and Patch scuttled away, and she burst into peals of helpless laughter. Luke gazed into her laughing up-turned face, his eyes glinting with tender humour.

'You're like a drug, and that poor beast is almost as badly hooked on you as I am.' He brushed her lips with his. 'Okay, *liefje*, you win. I'll compromise. I gave up the laboratory for my sister; now I'll go back to work in a laboratory to suit my wife. Maybe that way we'll make a go of it.'

'And I'll give up my country estate for my husband.' His brows shot up and she said hastily: 'Oh,

not to Henry and Delia—never! Father wanted it
to go to the National Trust eventually. And that's
what I'll do as soon as your friend, the lawyer in
London, can arrange it legally—with all the revenue
from the farms and other investments for its up-
keep. Perhaps,' she ventured wistfully, 'you'll come
and see my home with me sometimes?'

'Sure.' He ran a gentle thumb over her mouth
and she caught and held it and asked softly: 'Luke,
what does *liefje* mean? I've been dying to know!'

His eyes twinkled. 'It's Dutch, and according to
my grandmother who used to call me *liefje*, it means
"darling" or "sweetheart". Satisfied?'

'Mm-mm.' She turned his hand over to plant a
kiss on it and the glitter of his watch drew his eye.
'God! Is that the time? Narayan's men must be
rested up and ready to go. We've got an hour to get
out of here.' He was on his feet swiftly, hauling her
up with him and calling to Kunwar who had left
them together earlier, with admirable discretion,
and joined the muleteers and the guide on the other
side of the stream.

While they washed and changed, the servant prepared a makeshift meal, and while they ate it the
camp was dismantled and cleared. Selina was sub-
limely happy, and ravenous; anything tasted good.
Luke told her that he knew the British High Com-
missioner in Delhi and would explain the situation
to him. 'By the time we get back, you'll be of age,
won't you?'

'I've lost track of dates, even what day this is!
Yes, I will, I think!'

'Right. I guess I can persuade them to give you
house room and help me fix a legal marriage cere-

mony. You look pretty scruffy, my love, you'll have to kit yourself out.'

'Look who's talking!' she retorted haughtily, her eyes laughing at him.

'I reckon I'm no tailor's dummy. When we both look civilised again I'll take you back to England and make Spender and that harpy stepmother of yours wonder what hit 'em. Yeah, I'm going to enjoy that,' he concluded trenchantly.

The muleteers set off with the guide along the barely discernible path through the forest. Kunwar Singh was holding the saddled pony and the dog.

'Let's go! They're waiting for us at the pass.' Luke picked her up and swung her across the stream. The thought of having to travel with a crowd of guards and shackled prisoners upset her for a moment. She wanted——

'Luke....' she began diffidently. 'Could we go back to Mountain Water Valley—just for a day or so to see it again? Just us? It was so beautiful, so peaceful in the hills, with the village and fields and flowering trees, and goat bells, and black buffaloes wading in the river. I was so happy that day there. We'll never get another chance....'

He looked down into the round violet eyes pleading with him. 'You'd be willing to tackle the escarpment downhill, and the tiger's territory again?' he asked blandly. His eyes narrowed into a mocking gleam. 'Not to mention being alone with me? Reckless, aren't you, Miss Roxley?'

The memory of that track was daunting, but she shrugged: 'Why not?'

'Take that look off your face!' he chuckled. 'Okay, we don't have to go by the short cut this time.

There's a good track round, and I guess Narayan can spare us for a couple of days. We'll meet him at Ranikhet.'

She hugged him with joyful abandon. Luke bent over her. 'George Meredith, the British novelist, wrote a poem for us once.' He laughed. 'Called "Love in a Valley"!' Turning her from his arms towards the trail, he quoted:

'Cows flap a slow tail knee-deep in the river,
Breathless, given up to sun and gnat and fly.
Nowhere is she seen; and if I see her nowhere,
Lightning may come, straight rains and tiger sky.'

Harlequin Presents...

The beauty of true romance...

The excitement of world travel...

The splendor of first love...

unique love stories for today's woman

Harlequin Presents…
novels of honest,
twentieth-century love,
with characters who
are interesting, vibrant
and alive.

The elegance of love…
The warmth of romance…
The lure of faraway places…

Four new novels, every
month — wherever
paperbacks are sold.

Do you have a favorite
Harlequin author?
Then here is an
opportunity you must
not miss!

HARLEQUIN OMNIBUS

Each volume contains
3 full-length compelling
romances by one author.
Almost 600 pages of
the very best in romantic
fiction for only $2.75

A wonderful way to collect
the novels by the Harlequin
writers you love best!